PEACHES O'DAY

AMINA HARRISON

PEACHES O'DAY Amina Harrison

PLANET EARTH,
Baltimore, Maryland

CHAPTER 1

"PEACHES, OH PEACHES," shouts a woman in her sixties while she is outside the backyard of an old, like house one in need of painting even though the inside of the house, the family known as the O' Day family usually will do their best to keep their four room house livable. The people, who are living in the O' day household is a grandmother, the one calling out for another relative, who is the granddaughter also the mother of the one, as of now is calling out the daughter Peaches. "Where is that girl?" The grandmother says to her and although she has been waiting for Peaches to come home soon the grandmother will become little frantic. However, the grandmother by the name of Lucille has a right to become anxious when her family members not home at the appointed time. Living in now the 1960's Baltimore, Maryland; grandma Lucille sometimes wonders if there could be another place, in time perhaps on a different world, grandma Lucy as she is sometimes known as will leave Baltimore and its prejudice also injustices reeks throughout the city especially if you were a black family like the O' day one.

Grandma Lucy will sign, before she will start to pray only in the case if anything has happened to her only granddaughter, walking into the house all of a sudden grandma Lucy will hear the shouts of her granddaughter also she is running up to the house.

"Here grandma," a child of nine years old runs up to the house, her thick, soft hair is all tumbled on her face, and her clothes are little dirty.

"Where have you been? I have been calling for you?" Grandma Lucy says, even though at the moment she is hugging her granddaughter, Peaches for lots of reasons of living in Baltimore.

Now, Peaches along with her grandma Lucy will walk into the house as, both relatives are walking into the kitchen, Peaches will sit down at the dining table one brought by one of her mother's suitors at the moment, Peaches will see her favorite meal is on the table. Two sandwiches made with sliced, spiced bologna with also a slice of cheese and a piece of apple pie on a separate plate and for the granddaughter to eat along with the meal; a cold, glass of milk.

"Before you sit down and eat *G-d's* food, you better go to wash up," grandma Lucy says, suddenly Peaches O' day will hurry to the bathroom a smaller one even though he has a sink, and a tub beside a toilet the item stops up most of the time more than it flushes. As soon as Peaches had finished washing up for her lunchtime, the granddaughter will hurry to the kitchen to eat, and talk to her beloved grandmother, the woman Peaches even at her young age, hope the grandma will live for *hundreds* of years.

"You eat every bit of *G-d's* food, there is no telling when your mama will be coming home later," grandma Lucy says, and although Peaches usually her as her grandmother refers everything to *G-d,* the name at times confuses Peaches most of all when the granddaughter, and whenever the mother is, home are in the living room watching a used, television set though one found by grandma Lucy whiles she was outside talking on of her walks only to come on a house appearing as if the people lived inside had moved out. Stopping in front of the empty house, Grandma Lucy will look down at the trash bin, and her eyes had seen the nineteen inch television. "Will it work grandma?" Peaches had asked on the day her grandmother all sweaty from carrying the television had responded with a yes, also a hope so of words. After grandma Lucy found a place in the living room to place the television followed by the grandmother plugging the device in all of a sudden the television did work as of now the only real pleasure as well as expense in the O' day household is the nineteen inch, black and white television.

"I will be glad when mama comes, home," Peaches says as she will not start to eat her second bologna and cheese sandwich, right now grandma Lucy turnaround from the kitchen sink of where Lucy was washing dishes, as her grandmother sometimes do when she worries; Lucy will look at her only granddaughter with compassion.

"She will be home soon, don't you worry," is all grandma Lucy says now attending to the cleaning of the dishes, when Peaches has finished eating she will get up from the table to carry her dishes to the kitchen sink of where her grandmother Lucy is washing the other dishes already. "Grandma, when I grow up; I want to have my own house and wash dishes," Peaches says with a cutesy like smile on her rich, embrown face.

"I hope when you are all grown up Peaches, the white folks of this world will show some common sense with us black folks," Grandma Lucy says, now the dishes will be all cleaned.

"You wish Grandma Lucy; there are other worlds?" Peaches ask her grandmother at the moment the grandchild is sitting down again at the table to finish her glass of milk. Maybe because of the question Peaches has asked her dear grandmother, Lucille is not able to answer the particular one, and as soon as Peaches has finished her cold glass of milk, grandma Lucy will remind Peaches to go to the bathroom again to bathe, and get dressed for bed. As soon as Peaches is finished with her toiletry for the evening, the nine year old child will hurry to the living room to turn on the television the one found in a neighbor's trash can, and as the thing hums as it turns on right now Peaches will see a movie is coming on the television. Soon, grandma Lucy will walk into the living room breathing somewhat heavy like most of all when grandma Lucy is finished on one of her daily walks, however, as of lately grandma Lucy has not been out walking too much even though Peaches do not understand why, maybe one day Peaches will for after all growing up in the town her grandmother notes as, *the one dangerous for any one born with a black coloring to the bodies.*

"What are you watching child?" Grandma Lucy asks, as she is reclining her head back on the sofa one brought at one of those retail shops selling used, and old items as of now the store supplies most of the things, the O' Day family needs for a day-today survival; towels, old ones though, pieces of used furniture some dishes, and pots, and pans having the appearance as if the pots, and pans were sent to the used, retail shop from a nearby plantation in Baltimore, an abandoned one to say the least.

"One of my favorite movies. Big, eyes creatures on earth trying to kill the earth people," Peaches says as she is looking at what is known as one of the science fiction movies.

"Anything else you would like to watch?" Her grandma Lucy asks even though Lucy has seen Peaches sits for hours in front of the used television set looking at images of drawn characters known as cartoons, however, when grandma Lucy wants to watch the evening news; she will send Peaches to her bedroom until, otherwise. Nowadays with the O' Day family living in the sixties, the horrific scenes of murdered black men, and black boys grandma Lucy considers too graphic for her only granddaughter Peaches.

"I like these movies grandma. Always its earth was creatures arrive to kill the people," Peaches says with her pretty, brown widen eyes looking at her grandma as the granddaughter explains of why Peaches likes looking at science fiction movies. As grandma Lucy looks at her adorable, grandchild; sometimes before Lucy goes to bed she will find her kneeling on her knees such according to whether, as well praying for her only granddaughter perhaps someday situations involving black folks in the sixties of America also beyond will be better, so least of all Peaches will have a fighting chance in the world to come perhaps out of Baltimore. Now, diverting her glance away from her granddaughter, Lucy will look at the movie still thinking of the time when Peaches was born. Grandmother Lucille never did truly know Peaches paternal half except Lucy seeing the man coming by the house to go out with Peaches mother; Clara June. As the courtship continued among Clara June, and the unknown man, who sometimes arrived to the O' day house wearing the finest suits any black man is able to imagine wearing in Baltimore at the time; until one blessed day, the daughter Clara June will find out she is pregnant with child, the father, who grandma Lucy believes is the suit, wearing man is the father of her daughter's baby, even though Clara June sometimes swears the suit, wearing man may or may not be the baby's father.

"Look at her; sweet and cute. You are blessed Clara June," the mother Lucy had said to her daughter when, after the birth of the baby, even though Clara June had decided to give up the baby–then again not because Clara June knew at the time despite the circumstances, her mother would have killed her if Clara June had given perhaps the only grandchild Lucy will ever have to be born into the O' Day family.

"I need to name her," Clara June had said the night the baby was born helped by the only, black nurse, who lives in the neighborhood at the time.

"Name her *Peaches*. Her skin is a pretty, and ripe as one. *Lord* knows you ate your share of the fruit whiles carrying the baby," grandma Lucy had said as Clara June cuddle her baby, though it is true all the time of Clara June carrying her baby, the grandmother would have to go to a nearby, peach grown now almost died out because of neglect and glean the fruit for her pregnant daughter. It will be the sound of the television with the noise and as grandma Lucy stops her reminiscing, she will see one of those extra, extra large head characters, with the huge eyes shooting down a white man in the movie with an outlandish looking gun, as the creature with the big head and huge eyes are saying some unrelated like words. "I like this movie; the white one kill *a man* like those scary looking ones," grandma Lucy says as she laughs as the creature, with the big head, and huge eyes run pointing out his gun of fire rays killing off the *white people* in the movie.

"It's an alien, who is trying to kill off the people on planet earth," Peaches says as she will look at her mother in a curious like way.

"We need some aliens here in Baltimore to protect us," Grandma Lucy says.

"Grandma, I thought you said killing is wrong in the bible," Peaches says as she is looking at her mother. "Cain killed Abel," the granddaughter lastly says.

"The bible is the bible; you are only looking at a movie," Grandma Lucy says to Peaches with no more words between the adorable granddaughter and her overseeing grandmother; soon it will be timing for Peaches to go to bed. As the granddaughter, and grandma are walking to the one bedroom of where Peaches shares with her mother, and grandma in walks the mother all bubbly and carrying four packages like gifts.

"MOMMIE," Peaches shouts out as she runs to her mother knocking the gifts out of her mother's arm.

"Hey my baby," Clara June says, and although her child Peaches are picking up the gifts one by one the child Peaches will tear the wrapping paper off the gifts. "I brought you and your grandma some things," Clara June says as the mother will sit down in chair opposite the sofa in the living room, and whenever Clara June has been out sometimes four, and five days also nights on end; the daughter will usually have to brace her to be ready to argue with her mother.

"Thanks mommy. This is pretty," Peaches says as she is holding up a dress obviously the child's size.

"She will need to wear to school on picture day," Clara June says, then now Peaches will lift another box the second gift, the child has opened and inside of the box is, leather bound bible.

"Look grandma, this is for you," Peaches says as she hands the bible to the grandmother.

"You stayed up and watched television?" The mother Clara June is asking her daughter and with a slow nod, even though Peaches is beaming because of the gifts now Peaches will be asked to go to the bedroom. "Was it one of those movies about aliens you like?" Clara June asks.

"I wish someday I could fly high in a spaceship," Peaches says as she will now put her gifts on the sofa of where her grandmother is sitting, and the bible is laid besides those gifts, but before Peaches goes to bed; her mother will kiss her child on the right side of Peaches face promising the child of how the mother Clara June will be in the bedroom to tuck Peaches in bed. As it is when most nights Peaches mother comes, home later or sometimes days later, the child knows maybe her mother, and grandmother will have a one of those not too loving conversations. When, after she has walked to her bedroom, on the certain night; Peaches will walk to a window in the bedroom the tender moment for the child, she will see the moon with overcast like shadow also there is faint image of one side of planet earth on the full side of the reddish, color moon. With her adorable eyes widen, Peaches on the very moment as well as especial night is having her first glimpse of what is known in the heavens spectacular as a *lunar* eclipse.

"You come, home at this hour. You smell of a hen in barnyard," Grandma Lucy says as she is looking at her daughter as of now Clara June looks as if she has pulled more than your ordinary one, nighters'. "You told me you will be working at the cafe."

"I did. I earned some good tips, and I met a man," Clara June says as she will now remove her red, blouse a signal the daughter will be taking a bathe in the bathroom and maybe leaving her mother to seethe.

"So what? He would not anything but leave you again; but how much?" The

grandmother wills says right now she lifts the new bible and is now holding the book.

"Enough to keep us feed for a month, and pay the bills," Clara June says as she will after removing her blouse, the daughter will lift her purse next she opens the purse to give to her mother an amount in cash of almost three hundred dollars. "Earn every dime. Chuck's Cafe was full for the past three nights. He said the next time, I work overtime; I could bring home the extra, fried catfish," Clara June says now she is walking to the bathroom followed by the daughter removing her other clothes except Clara June's panties. Holding the three, hundred dollar bills in

her hand now grandma Lucy will stand up from the chair and walk to the bathroom at the moment, her daughter Clara June is in the bathtub.

"Remember, the good Lord watches us all," the mother Lucy says, now Clara June will look at her mother as the bubble bath, Lucy had brought at one of those five, and dime stores in downtown Baltimore one Saturday afternoon.

"Do not worry, mama. Remember the Lord loves the women. Remember of what you taught me when we used to go to church before the Klan burned it down?" Clara June says, now the mother Lucy will remind her daughter only to remember, at

the moment before Lucy leaves her daughter, she will tell Clara June regardless of anew man in her daughter's life or not; Peaches stays home. Afterwards, Grandma Lucy will walk to the living room again to stash the three hundred, dollars in cash in the brand new bible her daughter brought, home as a gift. After the conversation, Clara June after her bathing will get out of the tub to dry off her body next she puts on her nightgown the cotton one, also Clara June wishes she had brought home some of the left over, fried catfish from the restaurant knew as Chuck's Cafe where Clara June works as one of the favorite like waiter of

Chucks. Clara June knows because of her age of

26, as well as a grown woman, the mother of the child Peaches know she really do not have to account for too much of her life to her mother excepts if Peaches is involved by now; grandma Lucy wills do her best to make sure her daughter Clara June will not expose Peaches to the daughter's seedy side of Clara June making a living for her daughter. At the moment, Clara June realizes she is now hungry also she wishes she had asked Chucks for some of the fried, spicy catfish after Clara June walks to the kitchen; she will hear her mother watching the *television evens though grandma Lucy could be falling asleep. Looking into the opened refrigerator, Clara June will see the appliance is almost empty except for the few bowls of leftovers now Clara June will observe the plastic canister lifting it out of the refrigerator, the daughter will see, slices of cold, spicy bologna and slices of cheese beside the other cold cut of meat. Shaking her head signaling Clara June has not taste for the luncheon meats, at the moment also overlooking her growling stomach; Clara June will walk to the one bedroom she shares with her only daughter, Peaches also her mother Lucille,*

"Are you asleep Peaches?" Clara June asks as she is walking to one of the twin beds in the bedroom, also the grandmother and Clara June sleeps in the other two.

"A little mommy," Peaches says as the child will sit up in bed, and now Peaches are glad her mother is, home.

"Like your gifts?" Clara June asks.

"Yes mommy," Peaches says, now Clara June will explain to her child of how the mother believes the grandmother is not made at the mother. "Tell you what; before I go to work Saturday; I will walk with you to Miss Virgil's for ice cream," Clara June says as Peaches exclaims with

happiness her mother wills take Peaches to Miss Virgil's house the woman a widow, who lives in the neighborhood of where the O' day family lives also Miss Virgil is known for preparing homemade, ice cream for the children in the O' day neighborhood so the black children there will not have to go to a creamery in downtown Baltimore owned by a white business person, who may not serve any of the black children.

"Time for you to go to bed," Clara June says but before Peaches go to sleep, the mother will ask her child of what Peaches would like to be when the child grows up.

"An astronaut," Peaches says her eyes gleaming in the eventide of the day in the bedroom.

"A what?" Clara June asks now Peaches will explain of one day of how the child wants to be one of those she sees in her movies traveling all over space until the astronaut meets aliens with humongous like heads, and oversized eyes. "I believe you should become a schoolteacher," Clara June says now Peaches will recline on her bed to go to sleep, now Clara June will walk over to the one twin bed she sleeps, but before Clara June gets into bed; she will look at her only daughter Peaches recalling during the days, and nights when

Clara June spent her time with Peaches out of range father; he would talk sometimes in the strangest of ways.

"Where is my check?" The now older, grandma Lucille is asking her daughter Clara June as, both women are in the living room of a new like house the one with two extra rooms.

"In my purse; I would cash it for you, but you will have to go to the bank with me," Clara June says as she is now sipping on a new wine, Clara June brought off a street vender also Clara June as she is looking at her mother, the daughter will wonder if Peaches will make up her mind to do better with her life evens though, after all the years passed by, and now Peaches are at the age of sixteen seemingly about to finish high school; Clara June though has been thinking of moving out Baltimore later on coming back to the city for Peaches if Clara June will be able to find a nursing home for her mother Lucille. Nowadays, Clara June is more of a struggling single, mother since the day when Clara June had found out her backdoors like lover man is a married one. Sipping on the berry, flavored wine; Clara June evens now assumes by now the mother would have been pretty messed up if Clara June had brought Peaches to the bus station in downtown

Baltimore and wait for a bus and travel to another city to go to live with Clara June the mother, also the mother's supposedly rich, new man. It will be on the day when Clara June had believed she will be wedded to a wealthy man suddenly as she was standing in the terminal of the bus station in downtown Baltimore; Clara June had seen the wealthy, lover man stepping into the car with another woman.

"Some us black woman have all the luck, or we have something better between our legs," a woman, who was standing somewhat close to Clara June the day the single mother had gone to the bus station. "She is married to one of the wealthiest men," the woman had said. Though, Clara June somewhat knew the man distinctly, the single mother had asked the other woman instantly at the moment; Clara June had realized the gent played her. On the certain day, instead of Clara June walking home, she had detoured to a bar to drink, cuss and fuss at any man, who had tried to come up on the single mother. However, coming home three days later all messed up from the beer drinking at the time, the mother Lucille had realized the crab dumped her daughter of a man, the way mother Lucy had described her so called, daughter's would be beau and groom when mother Lucy had been introduced to the man. Instead of wishing, and fooling herself; Clara June will return to the restaurant knew as Chuck's to work there until the moment had arrived even though the owner Chuck had told Clara June the area of land of where his restaurant stands, a buyer had approached Chuck to make an offer to sell the land and build up a new sort of restaurant since, as of now it looks as if the city of Baltimore is starting to change with the times right now it is the year of 1974. With the year coming in, Clara June's mother Lucy had found out of how the mother will be entitled to social security likes benefits in the quantity of three hundred, and eight six dollars a month with the mother, aka grandmother to receive almost five years of back pay having Lucille to buy a, much larger house for she, the daughter and now the teenaged, granddaughter; *Peaches*.

"Is it cashed?" The mother Lucy asks as she is sitting in her cushiony, recliner another piece of new looking furniture also Clara June had brought with the back payment of the benefits.

"Come to the bank with me," Clara June says.

"How?"

"By bus," Clara June says right now the mother Lucy will start a rant about boarding a bus all because the white folks still has the law to have us, black folks to sit at the very back, even though Clara June as well as the sixteen year old, granddaughter Peaches had told even grandma Lucy of how the elderly woman whenever Lucille wants to board a bus, the grand matriarch of the O' Day family has the right to sit at the front, if grandma Lucille wants. Right now, Clara June will tell her mother if Lucy signs the check then maybe Clara June will have the check cashed.   "Where is my grandchild Peaches?" Grandma Lucy asks as she is sitting in the recliner all relaxed, and her glasses the bifocals type are on her lap.

"Peaches is at school," Clara June says as she is now becoming bored despite the fact the bottled, wine made by a street vendor in Baltimore is tasty, and relaxing.

"You should talk to Peaches all about colleges. And, are you still bringing to her those magazines?" Grandma Lucy asks, though Clara June will explain to her mother about how Clara June has been talking to Peaches about college, as of now the mother Lucy is about to become an irritant to her daughter all because Clara June knows of the magazines her mother Lucy is talking about, the ones every now and then someone when they come to Chuck's for fried, catfish dinners even now some white patrons are coming; one of those white patrons will leave behind a science fiction magazine of stories all about extraterrestrial lives on other worlds. A concept Clara June likes about Peaches reading the science fiction magazines, the reading will keep Peaches at home, and not out running around with the too fast girls Peaches ages, even though it is becoming somewhat too noticeable at times Peaches, and her mother Clara June evens when the two is out downtown Baltimore, either the pregnant teenager, girl would know Peaches from the high school, the pregnant teen attends, or Peaches would not know any other pregnant would be, teenaged moms she, and her mother Clara June passes on the streets in downtown Baltimore.

"Every now, and then I find the magazines at work. Peaches likes to read, and reading those magazines the time will keep her at home with your mama," Clara June says, even though the single mother has found out something extraordinary regarding to her only, daughter Peaches. One morning before Clara June had gone to work, she had cleaned Peaches bedroom of the new house as Clara June was sweeping, and dusting; she had come on a spiral of sorts. Lifting the spiral notebook; Clara June will read, pages of poetry Peaches has written. On a different day at work, Clara June had overheard one of the customers make mentioned of how he is looking for poem to put to music, and he will pay top dollar for the work. When again, the singer had been coming to Chuck's for a plate of fried, catfish; Clara June had waited on his table only to find out some interesting talk with the up, and coming singer.

"My daughter writes good," Clara June had told the singer then one day with the permission from her daughter Peaches; Clara June had sold the up, and coming singer one of Peaches poems granting her daughter a good sum of five, hundred dollars. Because a mother's intuition usually proves to be right regarding to certain things, the singer, who had put Peaches words to music had sold his first record real well, then one day, the soon to be famous singer will come to Chuck's to meet again with Clara June.

"Damn, right you child is talented," the now soon to be known singer had told Clara June the day he had been coming to Chuck's, and the soon to be famous singer walked into the restaurant with two women on his arms.

"I heard all about it. The next time, you buy one of my child's poems; it will cost you," Clara June had said, invariably it did cost the up and coming singer for the next time, he had gone to Chuck's restaurant; Clara June made the singer give her a check of five thousand dollars. At the certain moment, Clara June will tell the singer if he wanted any more of Peaches work, the mother will try to find a lawyer. Since then, Clara June had not seen the up, and coming new singer ever since. After the sale of another one of Peaches poems little did the mother will ever realize, her only daughter will stop the writing of the poems, and soon Peaches will begin to write a diary of sorts chronicling about a woman, who has fallen in love with a space being from outer space also both worlds the woman from Earth, and the man from his world is now on the run throughout space in the alien's spaceship because, both the earth woman, and the extraterrestrial is seen as fugitives from both of their worlds.

"Soon you will be out of high school Peaches," her grandmother Lucy says during the eve of the Christmas holiday also as, both Peaches, and the grandmother is sitting in the living room; Peaches admiring the five fir decorated also there are gifts like ten under the decorated tree. As she looks at the decorated, Christmas tree; as of now Peaches are wondering where perhaps the extra money came from for her mother to buy the presents, even though she told Peaches, her mother of how one of Peaches poems had sold having the O' Day family to be blessed with the extra money for even as the time for the holidays.

"I know grandma; mama told me its time I start thinking about college," Peaches says right now she has stopped looking at the Christmas tree, and at the moment Peaches reach over to where a plate of cookies, she had baked for the holiday now she is nibbling on one of those sugary, Christmas cookies.

"Amazing of how you can eat, and not gain weight. You look to be thin as a bean pole," grandmother Lucy says also she is about to become little agitated all because grandma Lucy cannot eat one cookie all because the attending physician for the matriarch of the O' Day family had warned grandma Lucy to look after her; what grandma Lucille identifies as the *sugar*, or the medical term; diabetes.

"Mama said it was good I stay thin; makes it easier for her to buy my clothes," Peaches says now she is eating her third, Christmas cookie. "By the way, where is she?" Peaches ask right now her grandmother has stopped looking at the granddaughter eating those cookies, at the moment Grandma Lucy is averting her glance towards the ten, dollars five feet in height, artificial fir tree.

"She said, she is on her way out to a party," grandma Lucy says, now Peaches will get up from the sofa to walk to the kitchen to help her to a cup of egg nog, the beverage Peaches mother had made with only a little gin also for the extra measure of taste, Clara June had mixed small, chopped up pieces of spiced, canned peaches in the egg nog. " Your mama needs to stop acting like an old, cow out to pasture still trying to find a bull to mate with; she is getting too old," the grandmother says.

"This tastes good," Peaches says now she will tell her grandmother of how Peaches will go to her room, and wait for her mother to return home, for after all it is *Christmas Eve.*

"Help me to the bed," grandma Lucy says referring to the bed in the extra bedroom of the new home, grandma Lucille had brought for she, her daughter Clara June and Peaches. As of now, Peaches has her own bedroom, all decorated in different shades of the color of soft peach with accents like blue, beige and cream. After helping her grandma Lucy to the bedroom and helping the grandmother to bed; Peaches will sigh as she walks to her bedroom to write in her diary as if Peaches is the woman from Earth on the run with her space being of a lover.

Placing her cup of peachy, egg nog on the nightstand nears her bed; Peaches will lift the diary out of one of the drawers of the nightstand next reclining on her bed; Peaches will write another segment about the earth woman and her extraterrestrial lover on the run throughout the galaxy.

My alien lover Jabilo believes of how he, and I should leave earth–again. I told Jabilo I should stay home awhile however my space being of the lover thinks they're more soldiering from his world will be on their way to earth in search of us.

"We must go now Afra," my lover from a different world than my own says, but I

want to stay on earth least for a while longer. Now, I will ask Jabilo to come with me to a nearby forest because it is where he and I have landed in Jabilo's spaceship. I ask Jabilo if he truly loves me right now my extraneous lover will show me again as his thick, moving manhood penetrates deeper, and deeper into my furry, eve's cup of loving desire at times like now; I wish, Jabilo and myself are not in danger. As his hands feeling hot, and slippery like liquid fire is moving all over my body in fast like pace, I will find myself hoisted on his broad, extraterrestrial hips and his full, mannish rod feels as if it is becoming lost inside of my sensuous, cave of desire between my legs. When, after minutes of the slow movement of love between me, and Jabilo; we are both exhausted even though it will be soon time for us to board his spaceship and be on our way he is running from his world because Jabilo married an earth woman; myself on the run because my government is out to capture me, and my alien lover. Goodbye again earth; my extraneous lover Jabilo will have to leave earth even though our love will always happens as Jabilo, and I are among the stars still on the "run."

Finishing up a new entry in her diary aka story, Peaches is little amazed the word her grandmother uses of how Peaches are able to write the love scenes in her diary of make believe of an earth woman, and her space being of a lover. As she closes the diary to prepare for bed, even though Peaches had waned to stay awake, and wait for her mother Clara June; all of sudden as Peaches is placing her diary away in one of the drawers of her nightstand likes a flash of lighting; Peaches will see a bold, and bright streak of lighting flash across her bedroom window. *I can't be; a storm on Christmas Eve?* Peaches thinks, as she hurries to the one bedroom window of the house at the moment, Peaches will see the lighter brighter, and bolder streaking across the skies of Baltimore only to disappear below the horizon of the city.

CHAPTER 2

"Where is Kaysen?" An extraterrestrial named Lysithea is asking another space being on her planet as Lysithea when, after eating her breakfast; had gone out to find her father Kaysen, the sole monarch of the wandering star known as *Megaclithe*. The cosmos knew as Megaclithe is like most other terrestrial planets supporting life on its surfaces, the same air for any terrestrials or extraterrestrials to have enough oxygen to breath also there could be other life forms such as on Megaclithe, there is certain species of animal namely two like mammals, though the two animals do not produce milk, and three species of fish, though one is most of all a poisonous one and only lives in a pond located mile away from where Lysithea, her father Kaysen and the other aliens of Megaclithe lives in beautiful houses made of four materials; wood, aluminum and silver. As the alien, Lysithea is asking the question regarding to her father Kaysen, the space being looked at the sole monarch of the planet of Megaclithe, and right now he does not understand even now, as to why Lysithea has not taken on another space alien a mate, also produce more to the population of *Megaclithe.* The extraterrestrials are able to observe Lysithea is as pretty as the other females of the cosmos of Megaclithe; Lysithea's head is almost clean shaven to expose even more of her good looks, and her eyes glow usually at night adding more to her galactic like beauty.

"I have not seen the one, of whom, the bright light seems not to shine nor arises unless," the alien says referring to the, what seems as if Lysithea's father has the power to have the one of the brightest stars in the universe to rise, and shine at Kaysen's very command all because of what Kaysen had found out some ions ago when a group of other beings had arrived to Megaclithe from a different world knew as Earth as well from those extraneous group of space persons their skins were of a deep, like ebony the monarch of Megaclithe had gathered enough information regarding to the planet knew as Earth all because those persons from the terrene know as earth had left behind volumes of books for Kaysen to read in his spare times even though all the while Kaysen reads those volumes of books left, the monarch of Megaclithe's eye wills see the words of planet earth in Megaclithe's *phonic* wording.

Where could my father be now? She questions in her beautiful, yet shaven head as Lysithea will leave the space being of her world to go, and search for her father. As of now, Lysithea knows the extraterrestrial is watching her as she walks on all because Lysithea discern the male one, is like her father good looking, also the alien wears his hair likes Lysithea's father; long, wavy tied behind his board, chestnut back except regarding to Lysithea's father Kaysen, his hair is not so long only flowing to his shoulders broad still for an alien of Kaysen's space age, also Kaysen's hair is shiny, shimmery like silver like that of the native, silver fox of the Australia of planet earth. As she walks on, Lysithea do not understand as of now her beloved father has not taken on another one to love, and mate with considering the alien men folks of Megaclithe are able to produce well beyond the ages of almost one hundred of fifty provided those alien men folks are able to procreate with one of the female aliens like Lysithea except those females of Megaclithe must least of all the age of fifty in accordance to Earth's age if those *Megaclithians* lived on the water globe. *He must get over Amenata,* Lysithea thinks as she walks regarding to her mother, who had disappeared years ago from the commune of where the other Megaclithians were living, even though Lysithea believes one of those extraneous souls may have possessed Amenata's body when she had walked to the area of the planet of where the dead of Megaclithe are buried, however, since the time Lysithea still hopes her dear mother will be invariably found–*soon*. One concept if for certain, Lysithea like the others of the planet of Megaclithe understands the large, bright star like the one rise, and sets below the horizon of the planet does into shines its light on the area of Megaclithe are the dead ones are supposedly resting and having the far *right* side of the certain region of the creation to feel as if the entire area is like a cold, slab of ice. Suddenly, Lysithea will observe her father is walking towards the daughter Lysithea appearing from somewhere even though Lysithea believes her father Kaysen may have tried to venture to the banished area of Megaclithe, the far right side of the wandering globe.

"There you are," Lysithea says as she is now running towards her father to next hug the monarch as if the daughter Lysithea assumed her father had traveled to the far right side of the creation of

Megaclithe in search of Lysithea's mother; Amenata.

"You have been searching for me?" The monarch asks now he will release Lysithea to look directly into her almost glowing eyes like the color of the rich amber, all because the gigantic, burning light in the skies above Megaclithe is starting to set.

"I was worried," Lysithea says as she will now walks alongside her father so the two extraterrestrials will go, home to have their evening together, right now, as Kaysen explains of how he did not dare try to go to the ostracized, right side of Megaclithe, by the moment when

Lysithea also her father has arrived home, the daughter will chide her father into telling Lysithea more stories not only about the strange like beings from a world known as Earth, even though the bluish, green like round one is seen as if it is rotating around Megaclithe except, if the space beings of the globe was ever to step outside during a certain equinox regarding to the entire greenish, blue sphere will stop its rotation around Megaclithe seems like hours on end before it will start its rotation around Kaysen's world. *"You were only so small,"* *Kaysen says as he will begin to tell again the stories of at one time, he says to*

Lysithea as she is sitting with her legs closed together by her well formed, knees, and her beautiful face in one of her soft, hands while Lysithea sits on a cushiony, sofa; as Kaysen will talk in detail regarding to a group of other beings from a world known as Earth had arrived to Megaclithe all beautiful; four women and four men all in search of better place to thrive, and survive without their world of Earth at the time was running low on resources. "Of course we appear strange to you, but you are like the people on our planet knew as Earth," one of those good looking, women had said when, after she, and her seven other comrades arrived to

Megaclithe in a contraption able to fly billions of miles way out far beyond Megaclithe which is where the "astronauts," were at the time on a mission to travel to the planet knew as Mars to find out if the reddish one is able to sustain life.

"My kind and I welcome you here to my world Megaclithe," Kaysen had told the eight persons from Earth later when all eight had settled in well; all during the time when Kaysen had made the people of Earth welcomed, the monarch of Megaclithe will learn a lot concerning a planet the name sounds far, farfetched from Kaysen's ears. "Yes, we have other groups of people on our world, but it looks as if you and yours are the only," one of the men of the people from Earth had said to Kaysen as the eight from the water globe along with several other Megaclithians were entertaining the folks from Earth as the time moves on; one of those women will find her falling in love with one of the aliens men of Megaclithe, however the love she had for the alien had posed a problem for the two. First, the woman had to return to earth to give a certain space agency a full detail of the "astronauts," journey if, or not all eight had arrived to the destination knew as planet Earth, secondly, the alien did not want to leave his world either.

"Despite your world is not too prefect; however I would like to know more as possible," Kaysen had told the "humans, " from earth even though he was very welcoming, however there will be a time when those persons from the water globe will have to return home. After he finishes the story, all of a sudden; Lysithea will observe of how her father is appearing little sad like.

"I like those stories Kaysen, but no more," Lysithea says as she will stand up from the sofa and now the alien daughter will understand as to why her father wills appear as if he is slumping into melancholy, as well Lysithea will not want to hear anymore regarding to those *humans*, how had arrived to Megaclithe from another world knew as Earth with their four volumes of books about their planet as well as other items; diagrams of the way those flying ships are built on their world as well as four maps depicting all four corners of those *humans* from the water globe; *North, south, east and west.*

"Now, Kaysen; it's time to go to bed," Lysithea says right now, before the sole monarch of the terrene Megaclithe goes to bed; Kaysen will turn around, and say

73

something little out of the ordinary to his only daughter. As he turns and looks at his beautiful daughter with her shaven head, and her glowing, amber shade of eyes; Kaysen will exhale deeply as he will now tells his daughter Lysithea regarding to his solitary life before Kaysen reaches the age of one, hundred and seventy nine at the time when the sole monarch will not be able to procreate with any other female beings on Megaclithe.

He wants his spouse to come from earth, Lysithea thinks as she in her bedroom of the home she shares with her father thinking about the request Kaysen had told his daughter regarding to the sole monarch of Megaclithe to wanting to procreate to have more *alien* children. After hearing about the father's demand in a sort of way; Kaysen as she is lying in her bed where overhead of the ceiling, Lysithea is able to see starry nights every now, and then Lysithea will see other spheres of planets in all shimmering colors passing by amid the stars. As she looks at the glass likes ceiling of her bedroom; though Lysithea adores her father as of now she does not know of how Kaysen will be able to go to the globe knew as earth of which he had learned about years previously when a group of beings from the plenum had arrived to Megaclithe then again as Lysithea is tossing, and turning in her bed rumpling up the satin like sheets made from a fabric of a tree the bark of those strange trees feel like soft, smooth wood, the alien daughter will recall at one time when her father had told her about earth, the monarch had mentioned about the way spaceships are built on the terrestrial creation. *He had to found out from the visitors,* Lysithea thinks right now her eyelids are becoming heavy with sleep as she closes her eyes soon the alien wills have another one of those frightening like dreams all about Lysithea's supposedly missing mother

Amenata, who Kaysen had believed had disappeared as Amenata perhaps out of curiosity had ventured to the right side of Megaclithe even now the first spouse of the monarch of his world believes one of those souls wandering in the barred zone of Megaclithe could be holding Amenata for whatever the reason could be. When a new morning arises on Megaclithe the gigantic, luminous star known as the supernova beams down its warming rays on the cosmos, surprise to Lysithea; she did not have another foreboding like dream about her mother, after getting up out of her bed; Lysithea will observe Kaysen is not inside of the house. The extraterrestrial would not have the time to eat her breakfast at the moment hurrying out of the home, Lysithea will have a run in with the alien, who has been admiring the monarch's daughter ever since he, and Lysithea were only extraterrestrial babes in arms.

"I do not have the time to talk to you; Ninsun," Lysithea says as she brushes passed the alien on her way to somewhere on the terrene Megaclithe in search–for her father Kaysen again.

"I could help you," is all Ninsun says right now Lysithea will stop in her tracks turn to listen as to how, as well as, why the alien wants to help the daughter of a king, of one of the largest globes in the universe, beside the extraterrestrial Ninsun is in love with Lysithea.

"In what way?"Lysithea asks if only for a few minute as, both of the space beings are standing and facing each other to talk; Lysithea will listen to every detail from Ninsun of not only a way the alien will help another one such as the monarch's daughter, however Ninsun believes he not only has a way to help Lysithea build her spaceship as she mentions the contraption whiles she is talking to Ninsun; however, if Lysithea's father boards the flying ship to travel to Earth, then as well as only maybe Kaysen will stay on the cosmos of the blue, green surface until he finds his new espouse right now in the rear of his good looking head, Ninsun will presume as well as perhaps Kaysen will stay on Earth leaving his only daughter Lysithea not only to carry on the overseeing of Megaclithe, all the same Ninsun will certainly be by her side a dream of the alien ever since he had laid his eyes of the amber shade likes Lysithea, Kaysen also the other extraterrestrials. *A beautiful, and satisfying ambition,* Ninsun thinks mainly because the reason as is the alien had tried to approach Lysithea with the thoughts of as well as the feelings to match to marry the sole monarch's daughter, but at the time as well as moment, Lysithea's mother had completely objected, now Amenata's is no longer around to complain if, or not Lysithea will become the espouse of Ninsun. After he has finished talking to the monarch's daughter, Lysithea will thank Ninsun with a promise as well to meet the extraterrestrial at Ninsun's house as of now the alien, who is in love with Lysithea lives in his galactic man cave on the advice of Ninsun's still living parents followed by the promise in a moment; Lysithea will observe her father is walking out of the house of another space being.

"KAYSEN," Lysithea shouts out as she runs again to meet her father.

Are you are following me?" The monarch asks as Lysithea is now hugging her father. "Be not afraid my child; I will never go the forbidden, right side of my world. If your mother is now safe, whencver she comes, home; Amenata will explain," Kaysen says now he, and his beloved, extraterrestrial daughter will walk home as well; Lysithea plans to go to the house of where the alien lives all because she had met the one, who told the monarch's daughter of perhaps a way for Kaysen to travel to Earth in search of a woman to procreate with to soak up his *seed* into maybe the willing, and new woman's *terrestrial* womb.

How handsome he looks, Lysithea thinks as she is looking at her father now asleep when, after she, and he are now finished eating their evening meal. One of the servants of her father's house had prepared one of the meats of the planet in like a special way, all roasted to perfection and with several other plants like vegetables of planet earth all during the evening meal; Lysithea was careful not to mention her plans to go out to another alien's house because of interesting information the one known as Ninsun had promised to tell to Lysithea. Next, Lysithea will make sure all of the four servants are gone to their quarters of the home of where Lysithea also her father lives, the structure is almost built like a palace the way Lysithea's mother had instructed the building to appear. Closing the glassy like door behind her also not to make a sound; Lysithea will now be on her way to Ninsun's house as she walks on, the extraterrestrial will glance up at the billions of small, balls of fire even on her world of Megaclithe, those stars appear closer perhaps up in the atmosphere maybe then any other worlds in the galaxy. Before Lysithea arrives to Ninsun's galactic, man cave; she will stop and glance behind her to look at the far right, region of the planet as of now the alien shudders all because the gloomy, shadowy area sends chill up Lysithea's well, formed backside not wanting to stare any longer, as the space being hurried to the house of Ninsun; Lysithea swears under her extraterrestrial breath, another one of their own is staring as Lysithea keeps on walking to a certain, other aliens' home.

"I hoped you would come," Ninsun says as he looks at the alien, the monarch's daughter also the one, Ninsun hopes will help him with more than many, loving nights on Megaclithe also Lysithea fits well into Ninsun's plan of the space being and becoming avant-garde monarch of the cosmos.

"I am most interested," Lysithea says as she walks into the house of where Ninsun lives all alone, also she is well aware of the way Ninsun admires the smoothness of her shaven head, and the way the monarch's daughter is walking in the house of Ninsun. "What do you have to tell me," Lysithea says as she will turn around slowly to face the alien as Ninsun offers a seat for the monarch's daughter to sit for the evening to begin when, after Lysithea has made her comfortable at the instant, Ninsun will walk out of the living room area of his home suddenly only to walk in again with what looks to be five rolls of paper, the one invention the monarch of Megaclithe had come up with when one day as Kaysen was exploring his world, the commandant of the cosmos had stumbled on what looks like to be a field of the planet knew as wheat on planet earth. After gathering up some of the wheat looking plant, Kaysen had pounded the shears together at the moment those pounded; plants of wheat had turned into items like sheets of "paper." However, it had been his only child Lysithea, who will discover of how the wheat, like sheets of paper could be used when one day in the Megaclithians own language as well as phonetics; Lysithea had written words almost lyrical like as of now also whenever the monarch's daughter finds the time; Lysithea will be in her room; writing on the sheets of paper made of the wheat likes substance.

"However, first we drink," Ninsun says when, after he lay down the scrolls of the wheat likes paper on one of his wooden, and glass like tables of the sitting room of his house next Ninsun will walk into the sitting room again carrying a glass, pitcher of a brew following the extraterrestrial filling up the two glasses as Ninsun, and Lysithea drinks also he will show the monarch's daughter the writings as well as the images drawn of what Kaysen had learned when beings from planet earth had arrived to Megaclithe; when, after her fourth drink; Lysithea will talk of how Ninsun was able to take a hold of all of the information least of all from Kaysen.

"I only had to ask your father," Ninsun says at the moment, the commandant's daughter will see a sheet of the paper showing a strange like drawing.

"What is here?" Lysithea asks as she will lift the sheet of paper to have an even closer look at the drawing. Though, the brew is tasty to Lysithea; she will listen as Ninsun explains about the certain drawing is what is known as a spaceship. The drawing is made with such an amazing detail; it will have Lysithea not only breathless, however she now has an interesting idea inside of her beautifully, and shaven head. "Now, I know of what I must do to help Kaysen," Lysithea says right now she will observe of how closer Ninsun is sitting next to her.

"I truly love you; I will do whatever you ask," Ninsun says.

"I am sure you will," is all Lysithea says.

"Then come with me," Ninsun says right now the monarch's daughter wants to know why Ninsun wants Lysithea to come follow him somewhere in his galactic man cave. Without no more words, Lysithea will follow the in love alien and at the moment, her amber shade eyes are hypnotized at the way the bedroom of her extraterrestrial admirer looks all over the walls of the bedroom is a shade of bluish glitter right in the middle and one of those walls are a drawing of a circle. As she is speechless, Lysithea will walk closer to the certain wall of where the drawing of a circle is on the circle is, squares encircling

the ring is, images of the males, and females of looks like the two aliens kindred in weird like positions of "love."

"What is all of this?" Lysithea asks, right now Ninsun will tell his lady, alien love in waiting he hopes; those pictures show of what Ninsun and Kaysen had learned from the others, who had arrived to Megaclithe from earth.

"The visitors, who came here call it lovemaking," Ninsun says, at the moment or maybe because Lysithea's curiosity has overridden her mind and is now easing into her body sensuously, in a moment; Lysithea will be on top of Ninsun's broad hips as the alien is making love to

Lysithea as she rides up the Pisces during the galactic aseem moment. First, she sensed the slight pain; however the pain will be no more as Ninsun's wandering, full wand of extraterrestrial life is moving in, and out of Lysithea's galactic "phudi." When their instant, moment of sensuality is over, the two long time of waiting lovers for one another are laughing as Lysithea, and Ninsun are now laying side-by-side. However, she must bid her star lover goodbye until another moment also Lysithea, though, she has a now enjoyed, her first moment of love will not be deterred when the time comes for her to make the plans as well as seek out a way to build a spaceship to travel to earth, nevertheless, as she is walking home before the gigantic, illuminating shine arises over the terrain of Megaclithe; Lysithea will be for certain it will be she, who will be on the spaceship to go to earth not her beloved father Kaysen. The reason the monarch's daughter has settled even now the plans in her shaven head; one parent now gone missing is more than enough for Lysithea to in plain sight stand now.

"How do you propose to build a ship?" Another alien by the name of Maro says as he is looking down at drawing of what looks like to be a flying like contraption the drawing is now shown to him by Ninsun, also a friend of the extraterrestrial Ninsun also Ninsun had at one time confided to Maro the alien's love for the monarch's daughter, however Ninsun despite the fact he had occupied a night of love with Lysithea; Ninsun will still be careful all because he had assumed Lysithea's mother could be held captive by one of those souls located in the disallowed zone of the right side of Megaclithe, all the same Ninsun will have to pay attention to make ready to do the exact of what he had promised to do for the monarch's daughter.

"There is a way," Ninsun says as he thinks as his friend Maro is looking over the drawings. "We have least one tempered mineral on our planet." Now, looking up from the drawings, Maro will listen as Ninsun talks about the one, tempered mineral on Megaclithe happens to the glass perhaps maybe used to build window like on the spaceship; Ninsun has proposed to build for Lysithea for the monarch's daughter's father; Kaysen. "I will need more time to find other materials like a durable metal, the kind described in the writings I have here," Ninsun says. While Maro is looking at his friend, however Maro has been keeping secrets to his alien being a long while. Maro also have been wondering if, or, when the monarch's daughter wills take on a spouse to bear children following, however the extraterrestrial Maro believes somehow his ally Ninsun may have beaten the space being the loving punch by the way as of now Ninsun is talking more about Lysithea than the father Kaysen, and supposedly the monarch's attempt to make readying to blast off to a planet known as Earth, even though, now the bluish, greenish sphere has not been seen as of lately perhaps because of a certain equinox is happening in the universe having Earth not to be seen in the skies above Megaclithe.

"Ninsun; I will do my best to look around our world provided you explain to me of what material you will need," Maro says at the moment, Ninsun will explain no matter how long it takes, though not too long; his friend Maro may be able to locate by chance a somewhat hard substance needed to build a spaceship for Lysithea. With much said, and although Maro will not make any promises, however it will be in soon enough timing the friend of Ninsun will search around Megaclithe even at one time Maro had walked near the restricted area of the right side of the planet, but his extraterrestrial wit will not allow Maro to even think of traveling so remotely close to the exiled part of Megaclithe.

I wonder, Maro thinks as he will now be out searching around Megaclithe for a durable like substance to be used to craft of those flying ships that landed sometime ago way before even Maro was born, though his still alive parents had told Maro about the peculiar, like but comely humans from a world known as Earth. With all of the details his parents had told Maro, while visiting his friend Ninsun to talk about Ninsun has in mind, the way Maro's parent told him about a flying spaceship is almost like the exact one Ninsun has in a drawing Ninsun has claimed of how Ninsun came by the information regarding to *space travel* by the beings who had arrived to Megaclithe. On his way to search, Maro will remember not to walk to close to the exiled area of the planet, but as he continues to walk all of a sudden Maro will see something extraordinary though not too distinct. As far as Maro is able to make out with his extraterrestrial eyes, the alien will observe up ahead of him is what looks like a carved, out open pit. At the moment, because of the rays of the giant, illuminating sphere knew as the sun what is inside of the open pit is glistening a glowing, reddish brown color. Walking closer to the pit, Maro is in awe of the pit encircles like miles around with whatever is inside of the pit right now Maro is somewhat hypnotized by the reddish, brown color of the pit now he will walk closer to the pit and kneels down to touch like a wall of the pit of where Maro is standing. As he feels the area of the pit it has like a warm, but not too rough feel to Maro's left hand as he continues to rub the area of the pit all of a sudden, Maro eyes will be diverted to a flowing, jetty material coming out of the ground of where Maro is not too far only far enough for Maro to go, and check out what is the flowing, jetty substance is flowing of the dirt of Megaclithe. After he has arrived to the area of where the flowing, jetty *matter* is oozing out the found of Megaclithe; again Maro will kneel down slowly to dip his left hand into the oozing, jetty *something* and to Maro's touch the flowing, jetty substance has the feel of thick, liquid like now standing up slowly; Maro will assume as of now it looks as if his friend Ninsun may have all the substances he will need to build as well as project a spaceship for the monarch's daughter. Now, as Maro hurries to return to the village likes compound of where he lives with the other alien kindred at the area of where the forbidden zone is there looking at Maro as he hurries on are two pair of eyes staring until Maro is completely gone away from the region of where the extraterrestrial had found two maybe valuable materials Ninsun will need; an open pit made of whatever, and the flowing, jetty like ooze coming out of the ground of Megaclithe. If so happens, both Maro and Ninsun where on planet earth the two aliens would have found out the two materials discovered on Megaclithe is known as a copper mine, and petroleum by all means maybe used for what Ninsun has in his extraterrestrial head to produce for an alien woman kind, one Ninsun has fallen hopelessly in love.

"It will have to be drawn out," Ninsun says to Maro sometime later when both extraterrestrials had arrived to a certain area of Megaclithe so Maro will be able to show Ninsun the two substances the alien had found.

"Not only whatever is inside of the open pit feels hardened like but maybe whatever is flowing out of the ground of our planet could be used," Maro says as, both aliens are walking to the area of where the ooze

of the jetty black stuff is still flowing out of the ground. As, both aliens are there, it will be Maro explains with time as one factor and experimentation will be another one it will not be far too long, Ninsun because of his ingenuity will gather up enough other alien men folks to mind out the reddish, brown element along with another several others to scoop up, and bucket the thick, black stuff flowing out of the surface. When, after the building to the spaceship as well as Ninsun testing of what use the jetty, black and thick liquid maybe used for the spaceship with all of his common sense; Ninsun will take a gamble when the time arrives for Lysithea father Kaysen will board the flying ship, all made of the reddish, brown element also the thick, strong like glass of Megaclithe also the gooey, jetty stuff will be used like fuel to propel the spaceship off the surface of Megaclithe. However, if, or not a chance like for Kaysen will board the spaceship to find his next woman to mate with, yet Ninsun assumes the monarch of the cosmos may do anything for love alone considering of how as well as mysteriously Kaysen's espouse Amenata had disappeared presumably where the outlawed patch if located. Now, admiring his handiwork one night as everyone was asleep on Megaclithe, somehow Ninsun believes the monarch of the terrene may not board the spaceship what if Kaysen much adored, daughter Lysithea?

"I am doing all of this; for us," she says during the time of eventide when Lysithea had met Ninsun on a different area of the planet to look at the new spaceship also Lysithea has made plans to board the flying air craft. She did not contact Ninsun for days on end all because the monarch's daughter did not want to set up any suspicions from Kaysen even though, as of now Kaysen has not been showing any melancholy as he usually do ever since Lysithea's mother disappeared somewhere in the deep, shadowy region of Megaclithe possibly never to be seen again. One concept Lysithea is grateful it also looks as, neither of the servants of she, and Kaysen's house is aware or even suspicious yet above all Lysithea is grateful Ninsun had not visited her although she had come to his home one evening though not to make love to the extraterrestrial. Lysithea wanted to learn more regarding to what Ninsun had learned from her father when the visitors from Earth had arrived to Megaclithe. One of the main ideas Lysithea had learned the bluish, green cosmos has more life forms on its surfaces living and trying to survive among one another. Soon, Lysithea will be ready to take off from her world to travel to the one known as Earth with the hopes there will be one agreeable, woman on the sphere willing enough as well to return home with Lysithea for the benefit of Kaysen.

"There are enough women here of our kind; why your father will only have to make a proclamation," Ninsun had said to Lysithea the evening she had come to his house, and although Lysithea thought of the same reasoning; however the monarch's daughter is more than grateful she will have the chance to visit the planet of the unknown, yet astounding group of persons who were traveling out in space in searching of a different world than Megaclithe there the visitors from the globe composed mostly of water had stayed awhile evidently Kaysen has become more than in awe of those extraneous ones from Earth; so in fascination the monarch is willing to travel to Earth in search about the women who lives on the extraterrestrial planet.

"I have chosen to go for Kaysen. I trust you Ninsun; to not tell him even if Kaysen suspects or discovers, I have left Megaclithe," Lysithea says now she will kiss him next walk home to where Kaysen is waiting for her even though Lysithea had made the plans to return to the area of the planet next step into her spaceship, the flying contraption, a rich, reddish brown color all shiny with glassy like windows not to mention the inside of the space craft; thousands of blinking lights also sound gadgets ready for its new pilot if, or not she knows how to pilot her new *UFO*.

"If he should ask--," Ninsun says now he will be reminded again by Lysithea of how the alien is able to make the story right when the moment arrives for Lysithea to travel towards the green planet, right now the sphere is seen up in the skies above Megaclithe. *It looks as if no one trusts me,* Lysithea thinks on a new morning as the extraterrestrial is now asking out of her house on her way to the region of Megaclithe where her spaceship awaits for the monarch's daughter to board and be on her way to Earth. She is not afraid, however, because Lysithea had studied the star charts as well as the maps of certain regions on the usual cosmos to Lysithea if, or not she will come, home again all in one piece as of now the most important issue with the extraterrestrial is she completes her mission to Earth followed by returning with a willing, earth woman aka mate for Kaysen not matter of what his reasons. Before Lysithea boards her spaceship, she will move one of her hands to rub the flying contraption and to the monarch's daughter; Lysithea has not ever touch something so for her since the now gone, missing mother Amenata when on some nights the mother will cuddle Lysithea when she was a child to soothe Lysithea to sleep. "Now, I am ready to board," Lysithea says suddenly the opening latch of the spaceship opens suddenly out of comes a glassy, and wooden ladder crawlingly coming down to allow Lysithea to climb aboard. Holding her breath the alien will climb up slowly until she is inside of the spacecraft right now, as Lysithea looks around, she will see right inside the sounds, and blinking lights are still happening at the moment; Lysithea will see a chair made of wood, all crafted as no doubt Ninsun now her lover has created the chair specifically to suit Lysithea. "It is, time for me to go," she says instantly the wood, and glass ladder will lift up slowly back into the spaceship and the opening latch of the flying ship will close pokily. At the moment, Lysithea will look at the opening latch now closed, followed by the space being and sitting down in the chair of the *cockpit* of her spaceship. As she stares at the mission's board of her flying rocket, at the moment Lysithea will think perhaps her father Kaysen could have been the one to make the *trek* to planet Earth. Inhaling deeply, Lysithea will sit until she will now say another command.

"I am ready to travel to Earth," she says not realizing the ingenuity the extraterrestrial admirer of Lysithea has created regarding to the monarch's daughter's spaceship. Trying not to panic, the spaceship will sputter slightly before soon it will start to reeve up its engines to fly Lysithea anywhere she wants to go conquering the galaxies. Before Lysithea will utter a word, or cry the flying ship will slowly but surely sails up into the atmosphere carrying its extraneous pilot possibly to a new world. All the time of Lysithea is flying in her new spaceship, she will find out Ninsun has placed inside of the *UFO* a gadget like a *voice pilot* so Lysithea will not have one, fatal mishap on her space journey into space. After at first she has traveled billions of miles, Lysithea will discern she is about to become little jaded until the monarch's daughter will say another command?

"Now, Earth," Lysithea says as she is sitting in her crafted, chair all of a sudden out of the wide, front window of her spaceship the monarch's daughter will observe almost right in front of her spaceship is the targeted planet. Smiling, and positioning her in the pilot's seat within hours of Earth's timing since Lysithea's flying ship is in the trajectory of the cosmos, the extraterrestrial from the wandering orb known as Megaclithe will be making a smooth like landing on an area of Earth of which Lysithea, however knows nothing of even though she is grateful of how she has almost completed her destination; in search of a new espouse for Kaysen.

CHAPTER 3

"Mama; grandma is sick," Peaches says to her mother Clara June as the mother is getting dressed to go out, and ring in the New Year. The O' day family had one good Christmas holiday until the grandmother had begun to complain of leg cramps almost disabling grandma Lucille from walking around even with a cane, the daughter Clara June had brought one day when Clara June had gone to one of those Rastafarian like markets the establishments are coming up seeming all over the area of Baltimore with the most African Americans are living.

"She will be alright; I will take her to the doctor day after tomorrow. You watch over mama, Peaches; I will not stay out too late," Clara June says followed by the mother is now out the door all dressed in her brand, new red sequin dress and the high, heeled pumps to match. After her mother has gone out, Peaches will look in on her grandmother at the moment grandma is sound asleep perhaps sleeping because of the pain pills Peaches mother Clara June has been giving the mother. Now, Peaches will walk to the living room to turn on the new, television the item displays movies and cartoons in living color also somehow having the new, device is having Peaches feeling little more richer besides she, her mother and the grandmother are trying to make every penny, nickel and dime stretch from grandma Lucy's monthly checks. She will sit down on the sofa in the living room before Peaches decides to turn on the new television, however she will though do one thing such as to go to the other bedroom of where Peaches and her mother sleeps at the moment, Peaches will lay down on the bed followed by her reaching in the nightstand beside her bed to lift the diary out. Sighing, Peaches will begin to write in her diary a personal but too personal account of an earth woman falling in love with an alien from outer space. Private moments like now Peaches wait at the most having, her privacy to think most of all of what she will do as soon as she graduates from high school. Pushing the conception of graduating out of her mind; right now Peaches will compose a few more pages of her journal depicting her make, believe, fantasy based on science fiction like characters even though the last time Peaches had written in her diary the very same night, she had dreamed she was the lover of the extraneous space man from another world. *"Where are we my love?" It is a moment Afra and Jabilo are now on a new world and though the world is so much like earth, however Jabilo discerns there could be danger in the new world. Jabilo will answer Afra as the two are walking around the new world, the world appears like the new Eden to Afra, and Jabilo everywhere the two are walking around on the new world; Afra and Jabilo will see, trees full of fruits and vegetables and rows also rows of beautiful flowers suddenly, Afra will feel loving towards Jabilo. Stopping in the middle of their new Eden on a new world, Afra and Jabilo will lay down besides each other to make love as the wind blows softly in the new Eden as he moves his full, throb of a manhood in and out of Afra, the birds high in the skies above the new Eden chirps and dance as the earth woman, and the space man Jabilo are making love*--after this writing in her journal, Peaches will stop her writing because at the moment she will see what looks to be a shadowy figure walking past her window. Although Peaches grandmother Lucy brought a house in a certain neighborhood in Baltimore; Peaches as well as her two other family members are well aware of the offenses is becoming increasingly terrible in the neighborhood with robberies as the main of those crimes. Closing her diary slowly, Peaches will place the book into the nightstand after her writing, now she will get up off the bed to walk to the living room while there; Peaches thought she had seen the same, shadowy figure walking pass the wide, window of the living room, the outline of it she is able to see through the sheer, like cream colored, curtains. The concept Peaches will do first go to the other bedroom to look in on her grandmother Lucy followed by Peaches hurrying to the kitchen to make sure the door to the kitchen is securely locked.

Right now, Peaches is sensing her heart is about to bust out of her blossoming chest because of the fear Peaches is sensing, with the door to the kitchen securely locked; Peaches as she walks to the living room again will see the same, dim like figure standing still Peaches will discern the shadow could not be seen suddenly as if the *shade* had disappeared. *Mama is right. Grandma should try to have a telephone placed in our home,* Peaches thinks right now she opens the figure of whomever is gone away from the house. With a new thought in her mind, Peaches will turn on the television increasing the volume with the hopes the sound of a sitcom with frightened away the *intruder*.

"I told Mama Lucy we have to get a telephone," Clara June says when, after she has come home from an all nighter at a local nightclub to ring in the New Year. "Happy New Year, Peaches," Clara June says as she is staging to her bedroom to undress and have a bath. When the mother had come home, Peaches was asleep in the living room after falling asleep while watching television also Peaches wanted to make sure the intruder did not come back to the home. As he mother is in the bathroom bathing, Peaches will next walk to the kitchen to eat at the moment, she will see two plates of food probably the food is a catfish dinner one of Peaches favorites.

"You know *Peach*; write another one of those poems I could see and we could have fried catfish almost every night," Clara June has said on a night when she, and her daughter Peaches were eating a chili bean dish. Since her comprising, Peaches had not written any poetry all because her story of a Earth woman falling in love with a space man has taken over Peaches writing time, at the moment as she lifts one of the foiled, covered paper plates; Peaches will see the plate is overflowing with three, pieces of whole catfish deeply fried with fried, thick cuts of potatoes.

"Oh, I forgot I brought the food home," Clara June says as she walks into the kitchen and watching her growing daughter eat the food at the kitchen table, Clara June will tell Peaches of how much the mother is glad Peaches had watched over the grandmother even though the daughter had thought a robber was trying to break in the house. "Damn, I have a headache. Hangover. Peaches I am going to bed; watch over Mama Lucy," Clara June says as she will walk to the bedroom of where the mother shares with her daughter

Peaches. When, after *Peach* has finished her eating, at the moment Peaches will feel as if the house is becoming colder now she will walk to the heating unit of the house to see it is turned off. After she adjusts the heating unit to least seventy degrees to save on the gas for heating the way Peaches grandmother had taught her; the idea Peaches would think about regarding to her continuing her education after high school. If, and when Peaches makes, ready to attend a college, *Peach* will make sure the college will be located in another state one like the state of California where the weather seemingly stays warm the year around.

"PEACHES," the granddaughter will hear her grandma Lucy shouts out from the second bedroom almost scaring Peaches out of her eighteen year old wits as Peaches was cleaning the kitchen after eating her catfish dinner, hurriedly Peaches will go to her grandmother's bedroom where Grandma Lucy is trying to get out of bed.

"Grandma Wait," Peaches says as she will walk to the bed of where her grandma is trying to get out of the bed also at the same time, grandma Lucille is reaching for her walking cane. "Mama brought, home two plates of fried catfish," Peaches says when, after Grandma Lucy now standing with her walking cane will allow her dear granddaughter to hello Lucy to the living room.

"Bring to me some of that catfish," grandma Lucy says as she is sitting down in her favorite recliner, the one piece of furniture is used however it serves the grandmother well.

"The doctor wants you to watch your weight, and what you eat," Peaches says as she is walking to the kitchen to prepare for her grandmother a plate of the fried catfish at the moment Peaches places on one piece of the fried catfish, and little serving of fries. Watching her dear grandmother eat, Peaches sits quietly on the living room sofa looking at the evening news broadcast on the color, television set right now the newscast is all about a war in a country known as *Vietnam*.

"Probably will send every black man in America over there," Grandma Lucy says as she is eating her catfish with the fries.

"Grandma, who is my father?" Peaches will at last ask right now the grandmother will place down what's left of the catfish a small piece, and will now look at her grandchild Peaches.

"One day your mother met him; next he would be gone later on, your mother will give, birth to you," is all grandma Peaches will say, now with no more questions the main notion Peaches will always remember despite there is so little facts regarding to the paternal side of her; Peaches mother, and grandmother never did bring up nor argued about Peaches O' day missing father. "By the way; where is your mama?" Grandma Lucy says as she looks at the newscast about the war in Nam, now Peaches will tell her grandma the mother is in the bedroom asleep. "Glad she did not bring home a *stag-a-lee* with her," Grandma Lucy says now, as soon as the news is over a movie will start to show for the evening hour on the television station.

"A movie grandma. I believe one of my favorites," Peaches says while the movie is displaying it shows at the beginning a giant flying saucer as if it is traveling throughout outer space on its way to maybe Earth. Before the movie is over, Peaches will see her grandma has fallen asleep in the recliner again the granddaughter will help the grandma to bed as soon as Peaches had helped the grandma to bed; she will promise grandma Lucy before the night comes in complete; Peaches will be in the bedroom to help the grandmother to the bathroom to help grandma Lucy.

"You will make a good nurse someday Peaches," the grandmother says as she will turn over in the bed to go to sleep, however grandma Lucy did not hear her only granddaughter mutters something about not ever becoming a nurse only a good writer of stories of earth people fighting or living or trying to survive alongside creatures or aliens from other worlds besides planet Earth.

"I know you will behave," Clara June says to Peaches as the newly, graduate of Baltimore High School is preparing to go to a dance given by the black faculty of the school. Peaches mother had brought the dress on sale a deep, shade of blue formal one also the patent leather, high heeled like shoes also Peaches will wear her first pair of hosiery. "You look all grown up," Clara June says as she is looking at Peaches now not all legs because even at her age of eighteen; Peaches looks as if she could pass for a good, slim though twenty years old.

"I believe the Reverend Washington son maybe a good boy. Seem mannerly though," Clara June says as she is now walking out of the bedroom of where Peaches was dressing for the formal, after graduation dance.

"The reverend's son David; is real smart mama. David told me one day in chemistry class one day America will send their first black person to the Moon also America will have their first, black president," Peaches says as she is beaming about the newly, graduate by the name of David Washington; Peaches escort to the after, graduation formal event.

"He talks like he dreams a lot, but Peaches let's sit down again," her mother Clara June says as, both the mother, and daughter will sit down close on the sofa so Clara June will school Peaches regarding to the daughter watching over herself while out with a boy, for the first time. Since Peaches budding into womanhood, Clara June will not allow Peaches to go out on one date ever since, however the mother will make a new allowance by having Peaches to attend the formal dance supposedly with a preacher's son.

"I remember what you told me, mama. A baby without a husband brings about hardship and shame. Also, a small welfare check," Peaches says even though she always admires her grandma Lucy the way the matriarch looks after Peaches as well as the mother even in Lucille's old, like age. In a moment, the mother and daughter will hear the sound of a car horn right out in front of the O' Day's household as Peaches is hurrying out to meet David Washington to go to attend a dance, at the moment Clara June wishes she had brought a camera but she had only enough money the day the mother had gone out shopping to buy least for *Peach*, the new dress and shoes. *I will buy one someday, then I will have Peach to redress,* Clara June thinks as she will now hear her mother Lucy bellow out from the bedroom calling for Clara June to come to the bedroom with Lucille's medicines. Since Grandma Lucy's last visit to the doctor, the man had diagnosed the Lucy as coming down with an acute case of arthritis. *Maybe one of those old, folks home,* the mother Clara June thinks as she will walk to the bathroom to open a cabinet full of medicines and ointments, after finding the pain pills for grandma Lucy's arthritis, Clara June if, or, when she places her mother in one of those old, folks homes the mother wants her daughter Peaches to be well on her way to college.

"You are a great dancer," the graduate name David Washington says as he is now escorting Peaches O' day home in his brand new car one his father, the preacher man Washington had brought for his only son David with the hopes the son will attend a college to become a *doctor*.

"My mom taught me when I was little," Peaches says as her sense of how she is all grown up while riding in a brand new car with one of the most popular boys of her high school, though David has now graduated with the other students including Peaches. As David stops his new car at a red light while waiting at the lights to change, the preacher's son will now suggest a new idea least before he drives Peaches home.

"To where?" Peaches ask David.

"To *Mountain Lore* up there we will see the full moon out tonight clearer," he says as he will now take a detour to a place known as *Mountain Lore* the hilly, like mountain way out from the city of Baltimore and *Mountain Lore* is also the stopping area of where young lovers go to have a moment of love under a full Moon if one is out on the certain night. As she will tell David of how Peaches has never heard of *Mountain Lore* right now it will not be too long, before Peaches and David are now seemingly at the very top of *Mountain Lore* the region is all hilly with various sizes of rocks, and stumble of thick like grass even though the two cannot see the city limits of Baltimore, the place known as *Mountain Lore* looks only to be one, not too towering hill.

"Sit close to me Peaches," David says even though at the moment, Peaches is looking at the full, orangey celestial neighbor in the skies above *Mountain Lore* also Baltimore. "Come on; I won't bite."

" I did not think so," Peaches says right now she will move closer to the handsome boy in her graduating class now, suddenly David the preacher's son will start to lick in, and out of Peaches right ear followed by David moving one of his hands to her knee also the hand is moving up Peaches dress.

"Stop," is all Peaches say as she is trying to move the roaming hand of David Washington away from her now rise up Peaches dress.

"Do not tell me you have not did it before," David says and right now Peaches will tell the preacher's son it is none of David's business if Peaches did it or not.

"My mama said a baby without a husband produce a bad welfare check," Peaches says at the moment, the preacher's son David will try forcefully to move his same hand up farther up Peaches dress moving faster alongside the right thigh suddenly Peaches will feel roaming hand of the preacher's son is near her still, virginal *clunge.* All the time of David trying to invade Peaches innocent *thullu* suddenly with all of her strength, Peaches will smack the preacher's son first in his face followed by banging his two, Russell colonels between his legs having David to wither in pain in his car.

" I WALK BACK HOME," Peaches says as she steps out of the car slamming the car door shut loudly as she is walking home from Mountain Lore, all the time of

Peaches walking she had thought she had heard David Washington mutters the word *B—tch* as she continues to walk to find her way back home. Grateful to be out of the horny, graduates car another one, Peaches will remember her mother reminding her if, and when Peaches have to walk home do not hitch a ride with any strangers. With the light of the full Moon's light seemingly guiding her way home all of a sudden, Peaches will see the outline of what looks to be a woman walking and as the figure of the woman walks closer as if she is heading towards Peaches, the newly graduate one from *Baltimore High* will see as the woman walks closer towards Peaches, the weird looking woman is entirely bald and her eyes—those eyes appears to shimmer in the dimness even though there is a full moonlit night.

"Mam; I hope you have a car; I need a lift," Peaches says as the woman, with the light amber shade of eyes keeps staring at Peaches as if the woman have not ever seen a person like Peaches even though *Peach* will discern the woman looks to be like a black person like *Peach*.

"A car?" Is what the extraneous looking woman says with the bald, head?

"Guess you are lost like me. We better walk home together. This is Baltimore; you and I should not be out tonight," is all Peaches says as she and the woman, with the golden, like bright eyes and bald head though beautiful walks on until the two are in the city limits of Baltimore where it looks as if no one is out on the particular night.

"Here is my house," Peaches says as she looks at the young woman with a bald head and that unusual shade of eyes. "Where is your home?"

"I have no home; I come from a long way," the bald, pretty woman says.

"I would have you to stay with my family because Baltimore is unsafe for black folks to be out all alone," Peaches says.

"I have come from a long way; I will go back to where I came from," is all the strange, yet beautiful, bald woman says and now she will walk on in the opposite direction of where Peaches house is located. Watching the young woman walks on; Peaches hopes the woman will make it home safely now walking into her house; Peaches will tell her mother all about the preacher's son had tried to be *fresh* with *Peach*. Walking to the bedroom the room Peaches shares with her mother all the while of Peaches undressing to go to bed; she will hear her mother talk to the grandmother about what could have happened to Peaches while out with the preacher's son.

"Go to the preacher's house, and find out then slapped the hell's fire out of the son for trying to put a baby inside of Peaches," the daughter will hear the grandmother almost shout out to the mother Clara June, now, as she is laying in her bed; Peaches will think about the bald, pretty woman she had met on her way home from *Mountain Lore*. Somehow to Peaches, the bald woman had reminded Peaches of one of those science fictions like creatures, Peach had seen while watching one of the so called, *really make believe* motion pictures her grandma Lucy will identify the science fiction films.

CHAPTER 4

"You will never see that Washington boy again," Clara June says to Peaches as the mother, and daughter are in the kitchen eating also it will be soon time for Peaches to prepare for her graduation. As of now, as Peaches is eating her second piece of toast with strawberry jam smeared on the slice of toast, even though her mother Clara June did call the minister Washington regarding to his son David right now the horny, like teenage boy is far from Peaches mind. Although she is somewhat grateful her mother has taken up for Peaches, when the morning meal is over, and now

Peaches will prepare for her grandmother a tray of breakfast food all because grandma Lucy has not been able to come to the dining table for her meal all because grandma Lucy is usually battling her arthritis. Preparing the tray of breakfast food next walking to the bedroom of where grandma Lucy sleeps; Peaches will walk silently like as not to disturb her grandma Lucy as Peaches places down the tray of food all of a sudden, grandma Lucille will awake now she will sit up in bed right now grandma Lucy smiles at her only, granddaughter.

"Time for you to eat, grandma," Peaches says now she will walk to the bed and help her grandma to sit more comfortably in the bed.

"Your mama gave that Washington kid, and his mealy mouth father a good almost cussing out," Grandma Lucy says as she is lifting the coffee cup to drink her coffee not sweet, but full of flavor with a dash or two of milk.

"I did not hear mama cuss," Peaches says and now her dear grandma ailing as she is, will not eat any of her food until grandma Lucy will talk to Peaches more regarding to an incident with a certain, preacher man's son. While she is sitting on the edge of the bed: Peaches will remain, quiet as the grandmother will say of how much she is grateful Peaches had not been molested by the young man also if the incident had happened, grandma Lucy will tell Peaches of how the grandmother will go after the son of the preacher with a shot gun.

"You will not have to do that; I will never see David Washington ever again," Peaches says now with a nod from her grandmother, *Peach* will remain in the bedroom until her grandma Lucy has finished her morning meal, followed by Peaches getting the grandma's medicines so grandmother Lucy will sleep for almost the entire day. By the time Peaches walks into the kitchen with the almost empty tray of food, she will observe her mother Clara June has gone off for the day possibly to work at the hotel now of where Clara June works in housekeeper even though Peaches had written two more other poems for her mother Clara June to sell to pay for another utility bill as well as buy more groceries for the Peaches, the grandmother and Clara June. After the cleaning of the kitchen, and having free time to her; Peaches will walk out of the house to go out and walk around to think. Though, she will be graduating; Peaches has one desire such as to move away from Baltimore all because the city is becoming congested, and poor even though Peaches mother Clara June is working at a local hotel and there is the monthly checks every month the grandmother receives. Walking along the avenue street of the neighborhood, Peaches will see the same, old scenes; a man cussing out another one, a woman hurrying to wherever also children playing as they do not have a care in the world considering of where those children lives; poor, decrepit and a prejudice place; Baltimore. As she walks one, Peaches will take, note there are no other persons and the automobiles though not many are seemingly to disappear even though Peaches understand to come home before it becomes night time, all of the sudden Peaches will be walking on the dirt, like pavement road at the moment the sun appears as if it will not settle below the horizon of the city of Baltimore all of a sudden, Peaches will see something extraordinary though extraneous located in a field like one of which Peaches has not recollection of ever knowing or where she is now. Being careful now, as she walks, at the moment Peaches will behold a circular like contraption looks to be made of glass, the shiniest, she has ever seen on anything like a house also the circular, object looks to be made of wood. While she stands there looking at what could be a spaceship all of a sudden the door of the circular object will open slowly right before Peaches eyes walks out the woman, Peach had met one night as Peaches was walking home, the bald woman with the luminous, amber shade of eyes.

"Earth," she will hear her voice pilot say as soon as Lysithea's space ship lands on the water globe. All the while of the extraterrestrial traveling out in space, Lysithea had become little lonely, also there were the times as she was flying among the various, other worlds, as well

as stars including the cluster of one well known one the Milky Way; Lysithea with tears rolling down her embrown, lovely face will sense sadness maybe because the idea of Lysithea traveling all alone into what is known as the unknown, perimeters of outer space maybe the space being from the world known as Megaclithe, should have traveled with her father Kaysen or the other alien known as Ninsun; Lysithea's loving one on her planet as well Ninsun the creator of her flying ship would have been the most welcoming of company for the now lone, alien. After her spaceship has landed, slowly the front door of the contraption *will open slowly next as Lysithea looks around at the area of where she had landed on planet Earth on the moment the space being had not sensed loneliness. With her beautiful, amber eyes in wonder; Lysithea will begin her discovery of the planet as she walks on soon the lone, alien will arrive at what to be an area of dwellings as she looks at the people in the certain area looks almost like Lysithea by the shades of their skin tones at the moment, Lysithea will keep exploring the region until the alien will observe a house even then, Lysithea did not know as to why she had wanted to explore the surroundings of the particular house.*

Walking around the certain building as she peeps through the windows of the house; Lysithea will see a woman like her reading in one of those rooms and it looks as if the earth woman was writing, in the same way like Lysithea during the times on her world of Megaclithe. As she keeps "peeping" into one of the windows of the house all of a sudden, Lysithea will see the woman is jumping off the bed as if something frightened her, at the moment the woman will hurry out of the particular room of the house and hurries to another one, at the same time Lysithea will walk hurriedly around the house as if the extraterrestrial is somewhat familiar concerning the house next, Lysithea will observe the woman is now in the different room and she has a look of fright still on her pretty, embrown face. However, it will be when the lone alien will observe a moving, like object with wheels and bright, beaming lights arrive to the house and because the alien has not idea of what the moving, machine is with the bright, beaming lights; Lysithea will hurry away from the house to run to her spaceship.

"On this planet; there is different species of life forms," Lysithea hears her voice pilot say when, after the alien has explored a certain area of planet earth, later on as she was out again exploring once again the extraterrestrial had met the identical woman, Lysithea had seen earlier. "My name is Peaches," is what the earth woman had said, now during a third time; Lysithea will see the similar woman, who has come upon her spaceship and, before long, the extraterrestrial will assume maybe now she has found the particular woman on planet Earth could suit Lysithea's father Kaysen purpose.

It could not be real, Peaches thinks to her as she is still standing and looking at the similar, bald woman Peaches had seen the night she had dumped a boy, who had tried to make out with *Peach.* Out of curiosity as well as acting as if she is not afraid, Peaches will walk slowly to approach the bald, yet pretty woman who has stepped out of what looks to be like a flying saucer, the devices Peaches had seen in one of her many, science fiction movies Peach usually occupies her time to watch at home. "I remember you," Peaches says as soon as she is close enough to the alien.

"I remember you," is all Lysithea says at the moment, the two women one the extraterrestrial, the other one a woman of the water globe, next Peaches with her boldness will talk more to what could be an alien from a different world than Peach's. "I am not from any movie you speak of; I am from another world," Lysithea says when, after Peaches has spoken regarding to the extraneous, bald woman with the amber shade eyes.

"Hope you enjoy your stay here," Peaches says as she will now turn to walk home, however an inner voice deep within Peaches will caution her to stay and help the alien. "Tell you this; I will help you and I will keep the secret. If you are really from *Mars, Venus* or, wherever, you will not be known because it may frighten some people in Baltimore or even the government," Peaches say lastly.

"My world is Megaclithe. And, I thank you," Lysithea says right now the two women an alien, the other one an earth body will walk to return to Baltimore to a house where Peaches stays all the while the two *women* are walking and talking all of a sudden an old, beat up vehicle will drive by passing, and shouting out obscenities.

"What is a *nigg----?*" Lysithea asks as she looks at the vehicle speeding passed by.

"Never mind. Welcome to the hatefulness of earth," Peaches says all of a sudden, the very same raggedy, automobile passing by with the carloads of people shouting out obscenities at the two women will explode with the fierceness on down the road having both

Peaches, and Lysithea observing billows of smoke, the persons inside of the raggedy car screaming for their lives.

"DID YOU DO THAT?" Peaches shout out and look at Lysithea.

"I do not know," as the spectacle of the burning car is now gaining attention from the other people, who are traveling in the same direction. When, after Lysithea's visit with her new, earth friend of whom, the alien believes, could be the woman to serve her the commander of Megaclithe's purpose, later on as Lysithea is sitting in her spaceship waiting for a new visit from Peaches of planet earth the lone, alien will learn her *voice pilot* inside of her flying ship has an inside defense mechanism really works on the sensation of Lysithea's visit on planet earth or perhaps any other *worlds* to speak out   the resistance on the certain sensation if Lysithea could be in some sort of jeopardy.

"Are you sick with cancer?" Grandma Lucy asks Lysithea when the alien had come to the house of the earth woman by the name of simply; Peaches. Grandma Lucille was outside sitting on the front porch of the house when her granddaughter had arrived with a woman, who is clean shaved however the alien is also a pretty like person.

"No grandma. Lucille; this is Lysithea. And, Lysithea here is my grandma," Peaches says after the introductions; Peach will explain her newfound friend from a different world is only visiting even though at the moment, Peaches will not tell her dear grandma Lucy any more regarding to the extraterrestrial. "It's a new hairstyle," Peaches says before she, and Lysithea will go into the house so Peaches will have an even more talk with the alien as well *Peach* wants to try to school the space being and regarding to the area of earth of where Peaches lives; Baltimore, Maryland.

"You young folks nowadays. First, your hair all over your heads calling it Afros, now the bald look as if you are sick with something. Your mama is gone out. Go to kitchen and cook me something," Grandma Lucy says to Peaches.

"She has to work late?" Peaches ask, now Grandma Lucy will explain of how she do not know if Clara June is working or whatever. Now, Peaches and Lysithea will walk into the house but before the alien walks inside of the house where the earth woman by the name of Peaches, the grandma will hold out one of her hands to shake the extraterrestrials.

"What; you afraid to shake my hand?" Grandma Lucy asks now Lysithea will extend out one of her slim hands to do likewise; all of a sudden the grandmother will have the awareness of not feeling so hungry. While grandma Lucy is sitting outside on the porch of the house, at the moment Peaches as she is preparing in the kitchen to cook as her new, alien friend is sitting in one of the dining room chairs of the room, *Peach* will as she cooks will begin her questioning of the space being only to have Lysithea to answer all of those questions with the up most truth the alien is able to do at the m moment. "If anyone did not know any better; they probably would have thought you are crazy or something," Peaches says as she will place the fried chicken into the oven to reheat the remnants of the food left from the previous night of a dinner.

"You saw me stepping out of my spaceship," is all Lysithea says as she will look of how the way her new, earth friend is working about in the room known as a *kitchen.*

"Well, I will do my best to look after you----," at the moment trailing off from what she was saying at the moment while in the kitchen, both women will hear the sounds of like a firecracker followed by a woman screaming then shouts of the people, who lives on the block of where Peaches lives with her grandma. Watching the earth woman hurry out of the kitchen to the front porch of the house; Lysithea will follow suit at the moment both women will see of what is happening is a riot.

"GRANDMA, WHAT IS HAPPENING?" Peaches shout out all of a sudden the young, black man will hurry out from nowhere screaming; THEY KILLED THEM BOTH.

"Help me back into the house. I did not see a thing," grandma Lucy says as Peaches helps her grandmother into the house at the moment, the alien Lysithea will be walking down the sidewalk of where at the moment people are shouting, screaming also a few of the cars on the block are now on fire and exploding. While Peaches are in the house speaking to her grandmother, she will learn the grandmother only saw the police car with two of those flatfoots inside, and, before Grandma Lucy completely sees of what has happened soon it will be an outbreak of the crowd of people. "Stay inside grandma; I have to go, and find Lysithea. She is unaware of what is happening on our block," Peaches says as she will help her grandmother to sit on the sofa and try to remain as calm. "Lysithea is from another world." Before grandma is able to protest to what in the world her granddaughter is talking about; Peaches is out the door hurrying down the sidewalk also she is careful she do not become caught up in the rioting of the people. Of all the years of Peaches living in Baltimore, she has a sort of discernment of what could be occurring. Peaches lost a great uncle, years prior before she was born according to Grandma Lucy. The older brother of Lucille was arrested one evening as he was on his way home from work only to be found days later dead inside a jail cell in the city of Baltimore. "All of Hoover's devils are going straight to hell biting their tongues," Grandma Lucy had said days after the funeral of her only and oldest brother. Now, Peaches will hear the sounds of more sirens showing more of the flatfoots are on their way to where the rioting is taking place, also Peaches do not see a sign of where the alien Lysithea, but Peaches hopes the alien could have gone off to her spaceship as soon as Peaches returns home by scampering through the crowd of angry people; she will make sure her grandmother is alright hours after the riot soon Clara June will hurry into the house somewhat grateful the residence her mother Lucille brought is still intact.

"A cop stopped a car with a black man, and a white woman inside. The cop asked the black man to get out of the car after that, the cop shot the black man next he shot the white woman, the two are dead," Clara June told her mother, and granddaughter of the details of the incident happened in downtown Baltimore also the shootings spurred a riot.

"It keeps happening too much," grandma Lucy says as she shakes her head in disgust though her granddaughter and daughter do not know; there are some *days grandma Lucille wishes she could wake up on a different world one where there is no white cops full of malice ready to kill any black person at any time. As the certain area of Baltimore becomes, quiet although the cars and some buildings are burning as firefighters are trying to extinguish the burning buildings; Peaches while in her bedroom had thought about going out and searching for a woman, with the bald head and the beauty with eyes of amber, then again Peaches will wait until the sun arises early to go to a certain fielding outside the city limits of Baltimore, and as Peaches opens the nightstand drawer to lift out her diary,*

179

she hopes the alien name Lysithea is indeed safe, and sound inside of her spaceship.

"Malice those life forms harbor against one another. Even the like forms of certain animals are ready to defend and killed the life forms known as humans. No respect for a world as almost as perfect as Megaclithe," the voice pilot inside of Lysithea's space craft says to the alien while Lysithea is sitting in her chair also thinking of the incident she has witnessed really the first one since Lysithea landed on planet Earth. After looking at the during the moment, the extraterrestrial had heard someone shout at Lysithea;

"GET OUT OF THE WAY NEFERTITI," at the time, Lysithea turned around to see a young man running somewhere another direction followed the shout out; Lysithea will hurry to her spaceship where it is located in fielding and even there the space alien discerns of how peaceful the region of Earth of where her flying saucer has landed. I will have to be careful, Lysithea thinks after the reading from her voice pilot, the alien will get up from her chair and walk over to where a large, paper sack is inside of the spaceship. Opening the brown paper sack, there is the foods of planet Earth given to Lysithea from the woman, the alien hopes will be

the one to return with Lysithea to Megaclithe now lifting out the two pieces of an earth food known as "fried chicken," as the extraterrestrial eats the food followed by drinking an orangey like drink in a glass like bottle; if it were not for Lysithea arriving to the extraneous world to the space being; Lysithea could have stayed awhile.

"I only return to find out if you are alright," Peaches says to Lysithea on a new morning on the early of it when Peaches had walked to the fielding of where on the spot is the spaceship with the gleaming, like glass windows. Before Peaches had made ready to go to the fielding, she is grateful her mother will stay home with her mother even though, before grandma Lucy awoke; Clara June had talked to Peaches about placing grandma Lucille in a nursing home for the aged. "But, why?" Peaches ask at the moment Clara June will explain because of grandma Lucy is becoming an ailing more, and more as well becoming older with no more talk about placing grandma Lucy away; Peaches will not hear any more suddenly Peaches will walk out of the house to hurry to the spaceship.

"I arrived safely," Lysithea says right now Peaches will try to explain to the alien all about the incident happened a day earlier.

"May I go inside of your spaceship?" Peaches ask now Lysithea will offer to escort the earth woman inside of the extraterrestrials flying, space craft and while inside Peaches cannot believe her eyes. Of all the times of she watching television about aliens from other worlds all the movies created with actors in a place known as Hollywood as Peaches walks around the circular, spaceship she will touch and ask all about the gadgets inside of the *UFO*. At the moment of her exploring around the spaceship

"Is something wrong?" Lysithea asks now Peaches will try to explain to the alien on planet Earth, there are men of the government agencies in America if word is out concerning the alien; it could place the extraterrestrial in somewhat of a great danger. "I will not return to my world without one thing concerning Kaysen," Lysithea says.

"Who is Kaysen?" Peaches ask as she looks at the bald, alien with the brightest eyes in her extraterrestrial head. Now, Peaches will hear from the alien the one known as Kaysen is the commandant, and father of Lysithea as the space being talked on; it will be what Lysithea will say will have Peaches thunderstruck let alone why another alien from a different world than Earth will want to marry a woman from the *water planet?*

"There are no way my people, who were a group of astronauts ever traveled out into space. The astronaut from America are all white," Peaches says then now Lysithea will try to explain to the earth woman of how Lysithea's world is light years ahead of planet earth in other worlds, Lysithea has already experienced the upcoming future of Peaches cosmos.

"Now, will you return to Megaclithe with me?" Lysithea asks now Peaches will tell the extraterrestrial of how the earth woman will need more time because Peaches is now facing family matters, besides if what is true regarding to what Lysithea has told Peaches; maybe it will be good for Peaches to depart from planet earth as well as be a witness of far in light years the plenum known as Megaclithe is ahead of the *water planet*. Without an answer to Lysithea; Peaches will leave the space alien to go home even though, as she is traveling alone, the time will afford Peaches to think about so many issues most of all Peaches mother had told the daughter the time is now the daughter Clara June will have to get ready to register grandma Lucille into a place so the grandmother will be looked after also Clara June is becoming little tired of taking care of Lucille, however Clara June has made new plans for her after the settling of her mother Lucille; Clara June will work on next helping Peaches to attend a college as well as live on the new campus. However, as soon as Peaches goes, home what she has been hopeful would not happen is happening soon when Peaches arrives, home to see an ambulance and her grandmother is hauled inside of the vehicle.

"Where were you?" Clara June asks Peaches while the daughter is standing beside her mother.

"I was out visiting a friend. Should we go to the hospital?" Peaches ask now, both the mother, and daughter will make, ready to go to the hospital by taxi even though Clara June cannot believe after the riots, a taxi will arrive to the neighborhood though the vehicle drove by a black man. As the mother and daughter are on their way to the general hospital to find out if Grandma Lucy will make it because the grandmother has been suffering from another stroke to her brain. After arriving to the general hospital, what is known as the *colored* ward of the building at the moment Peaches and her mother will see a good looking, black man walking towards them wearing a crisp, white coat?

"The O' day family?" The physician asks now Clara June will introduce her also her daughter. "I am sorry. Mrs. O' day did not make it," the good looking, physician says now with no more words even to her mother; Peaches will bolt out of the hospital leaving her mother on the same day when the time Peaches comes, home it will be almost the eventide of the hour. After coming home; Peaches will see her mother is not at home, and walking to her bedroom even though Peaches cannot understand if she is enraged or sad; now laying on her bed she will think about the offer a woman from a totally, different world from Peaches has asked the earth woman most regarding to the space alien Lysithea and the monarch name Kaysen, the commandant of a world known as *Megaclithe*. When her thinking is over, Peaches will reach over to where her diary is located inside of the nightstand drawer next lifting the book out also Peaches hopes the writing will take her mind away from the death of her grandmother, *Peach* will not begin to write perhaps the last chapter in her diary of fantasy.

"Looks as if we are back to where we started," Afra says as she is looking at her lover from another planet; Jabilo. As the two the earth woman, and the alien are standing and looking at ruins of buildings all of a sudden it will become all too familiar to Afra. The buildings are the identical ones located where at one time, the country of America's capitol; Washington DC.

"Your world looks as if it has been destroyed," Jabilo says now he, and his earth lady aka lover woman Afra will walk around what looks as if the city of

Washington Dc is completely bombed out either by a nuclear attack or perhaps extraterrestrials from another world has completely destroyed the city of where men, and women ruled by setting up laws in the best interest of their comrades know, matter if those laws affected the poor masses greatly.

"I am tired," Afra says her hair is still beautiful even though her jetty, tresses have been jostled by the traveling all over the universe with her extraneous lover as well as the moments when Afra will lay down beside Jabilo to enjoy a moment of lovemaking.

"Here," is all Jabilo says when, after his Earth lady Afra have found the building looks as if it had contained millions of books now all tattered and burned out having the volumes appearing beyond repair. Now, the extraneous one and his lover woman from Earth will sleep as a full moon arises over the city of Washington DC or what is left of the capitol arena of America.

"We will have to create our race of people. We could have a family," Afra says now she will move her soft hands all over the area of the body her lover Jabilo is exposed and now the two will make, love beneath a building almost totally destroyed and it is

missing a rooftop. As the days and nights pass on Afra and Jabilo will create a new race of their own for a new day to rebuild the earth.

The day of grandma Lucy's funeral was a bright, and sunny one all the time of Clara June and Peaches at the cemetery the mourners were commenting the reason the weather is so fair, and beautiful is because, when she was alive; Grandma Lucille O' day lived a life of the times when she would put her family always–first. As Clara June and Peaches were riding in one of the limos from the cemetery to go home and be ready for the guests, at the moment Peaches will find out her dear grandma Lucy had left Peaches enough money to attend college when Peaches graduates from high school.

"How much?" Peaches ask as she looks out the window of the limo while sitting the opposite side from her mother and what is really confusing to Clara June; Peaches had not shed one tear at the services in church nor at the cemetery.

"Five thousand. Enough; provided you do not choose an expensive college," Clara June says and although it looked as if Peaches did not mourn at her grandmother's funeral, however Clara June did though the cosmetics on Clara

June's face looks still untouched. Proceeding, the limo arrives to the house the building grandma Lucy had brought when Lucille had begun to receive her monthly pensions. "Try to smile *Peach*. So, the guests will not start to wonder," Clara June says as the mother, and daughter steps out of the limo right now Peaches will see there is already four or five carloads of people, who have a now arrived at the home of *Mrs. Lucille O' day*. All during the time the mourners are at the house, Peaches did not talk to any of the visitors even though all the time of eating and drinking the main subject was the shooting happened earlier before the death of Grandma Lucy. "Shame he had to die in behind the white trash," Peaches had heard one of the mourners retort the one, who had been the soloist at the funeral of Peaches grandmother.

"Plenty of black women at the church where I attend," a man, who Peaches had found out before the funeral was one of the deacons of the church says as he is eating a large, piece of chicken fried like all during the visiting of the now, demise Mrs. Lucille O' day's house; soon it will be timed for the visitors to leave as they all are walking out of the house with comments of "call me if you ever should need me," Peaches will go to her bedroom and only stare at one of the walls of her bedroom. Though she is grateful of how her grandmother had bequeathed Peaches enough money for her future, ever since Peaches had met another woman, from a different world than the one Peaches knows as Earth, the soon to be graduate from high school is now, considering on leaving the water globe–*and so what*? Thinking of too getting away *from the hate, and to kill any black person* in Baltimore; one concept Peach likes regarding to the offer the extraterrestrial had said to *Peach*. "Not only you will take the place of my mother; Kaysen have enough power as the commandant of *Megaclithe* to take care whenever you so desires to visit Earth," Lysithea says at the time; Peaches had found out from her space being friend, the wandering terrene known as *Megaclithe* has a percentile of the oxygen 15, and if Peach do decide to go with Lysithea the earth woman will realize all of what is happening to her is more than the brainchild like fantasy.

"Come in," Peaches says when she hears a soft knock on the door of her bedroom. Looking at her mother, even though both women are grateful the visitors are now gone for the day; right now it will be what Peaches mother Clara June says, will have Peaches to at the moment scream, and shout almost hit at her mother.

"I have someone coming over. A man I want to marry. His name is Clements," Clara June says.

"Wasn't he the one, who had told the police about the black man with a white woman?" Peaches ask, at the moment Clara June is discerning a little hostility in her daughter's voice. Though, Clara June knows Peaches is more smart than even the mother gives the daughter the credit, the only way Clara June assumes her daughter Peaches had heard something about the mother's new lover man perhaps from one of the old, gossipers grandma Lucy had heard from before the grandmother passed away.

"No one knows for sure," Clara June says right now Peaches will stand up, and push her mother aside all at the same moment, the front door bell to the house will ring. Overlooking her perhaps angry daughter maybe after the death of Peaches grandma, Clara June rushes to answer the front door and their standing is a man, almost as short as Clara June a mere five, feet a four inches tall standing and smiling with enough gold on his teeth as if the man known as Clements as if the love man of Clara June has his dental work at *Fort Knox*.

"Hey Clara June baby," Clements shouts out as Peaches brushes past the man almost pushing the mother's friend out of the way. "Was that your daughter?" Clements the gold teeth man asks.

"Yea. She is upset. I burled my mother today and Lucille was Peaches grandmother," is all Clara Junes says as she ushers Clements into the house overlooking the mere fact, the new lover in waiting did not bother to attend Clara June's mother funeral. Maybe because Peaches is upset at what her mother has pulled off, as she walks hurriedly to the area of where an outlandish, woman from a world known as Megaclithe is waiting in her spaceship, the wind is blowing like the warm mildness and the street where Peaches has been living mostly all of her life is now, as quiet as a horde of church mice. *Lysithea did say the ruler of the planet of Megaclithe could make any arrangement I please when I return with Lysithea,* Peaches thinks as she will walk onto the certain area suddenly she will arrive and their standing as if it is like a dream; Peaches will see the spaceship much like the ones Peaches had seen the times watching those sciences fiction movies. Walking nearer to the circular object suddenly Peaches will see the space being and climbing down the ladder perhaps to meet with Peaches as well as if the earth woman has decided to return to Megaclithe with the extraterrestrial.

"I hoped, you'll come," Lysithea says her amber shade of eyes gleaming like the gem. "My time is nearing for me to go to my world."

"I have made up my mind. You and the commander of the planet keep your promise," Peaches says aright now the alien will discern the earth woman is glancing up at the skies above her planet. "I would not have even imagined one day

I will see a person from a different world. I knew there is no life on the Moon."

"The Moon?" Lysithea asks now Peaches will explain as well as point up towards the celestial object in the cerulean blue skies also Peaches will explain in her day, and time only there are *white* men, who travels to the Moon. "When you return home with me; you will see light years ahead a group of Earth beings arrived to Megaclithe. Beautiful people like you, and they left some interesting information for Kaysen. And, it is why he wanted to travel to Earth, but instead I did."

"So, when do we leave?" Peaches ask right now she will learn in two days of timing; Peaches will be leaving earth to travel billions of until miles to another cosmos perhaps much like earth from what Peaches has been informed by Lysithea.

"Sorry for your loss," the alien says, then now Peaches will find out when the extraterrestrials on the creation known as Megaclithe passes on; their souls move to a dissimilar area of the plenum, a place of *darkness* never to be seen again. Now, the space alien will take note Peaches is looking somewhat horrified. "There is no need to be afraid. My kindred and I; lives a long time on our world," Lysithea says now the alien will observe Peaches looks as if she is relieved. With the promise to leave Earth in two days of timing, the earth woman will return to her home with no more questions regarding to Peaches getting ready to depart planet earth maybe one day return--then again, *who really knows?*

It's quiet here; she must be out with her man, Peaches thinks when, after returning home to see the house looks to be completely empty. The sun is starting to set, and she has not realized of how long Peaches had stayed to visit the alien by the name of Lysithea; now *Peach* will walk to the kitchen to see also there is still enough food left from the visitors, who had come to her house after the funeral of Grandma Lucy. Lifting a plate out of the cupboard of kitchen and now Peaches will prepare a plate cold ham, and sweet potato salad. Before she sits down to eat, Peaches will hear her mother maybe in the bedroom of where the grandmother had slept and Peaches hears the voice of the man could be the one name Clements.

Taking no thought it is the man; Peaches without eating now will hurry to the bedroom and as she discerned right in the bed with her legs sprawled out with the naked, wet Clements on top of her; Peaches will sense her becoming disgusted on the very sighting of her mother making love in the bed of her mother not even one day later from the death of grandma Lucille.

"YOU DIRTY BI–TH. GRANDMA WAS HERE; SHE WILL SET BOTH OF YOU ON FIRE," Peaches says as she storms away from the bedroom door.

"PEACHES," her mother Clara June shouts out as the mother tries to shove the lover man Clements off her naked body.

"Ain't through with you woman," Clements says as he moves his overblown, lauda though Clara June is trying to shove the lover off of her; Clements the shorty like camacho believes as he rides away on Clara June's full hips the reetchy moment is really a game. Perhaps because Peaches is sensing a sort of betrayed finding her mother in the very act of lovemaking, hurrying to the kitchen Peaches will gather up all the food left behind from the mourners in five, brown paper bags, and when the sun has fully set; Peaches is out the door holding onto the five paper bags on her way to the area of where a spaceship awaits, for Peach to return home with an extraterrestrial known by the name of Lysithea.

CHAPTER 5

"One woman–two worlds"

"It's called the *Milky Way*," Peaches says to her alien host as the two are on the spaceship the extraterrestrial Lysithea had arrived to earth inside of one in search of the seemingly perfect, earth woman for her father, the monarch of a wandering orb known as Megaclithe. While eating a piece of peach pie, the fruit Peaches had told Lysithea the reason the earth woman was given the name because, when Peaches was a child at the time, it is how much Peaches had wanted to eat the fruit as much as her grandmother Lucy, then alive would buy the fruit for her. Though, Peaches had decided to go with the alien from another world, one act she would do before taking off. A day earlier, Peaches had visited the grave site of her grandmother, the mound looks to be still fresh and while standing there gazing down at the grave site; Peaches knows one concept for sure whenever she do travel with the alien to leave Earth; *Peach* needs not worry really to return to earth for after all her grandma Lucy is no longer living. "Grandma Lucy; now I am so confused. I do not know if to stay mad because you died or stay upset at mama.

All the time you lived with us; mama talked of placing you in a home for old folks, and I would not let her. Well, grandma; remember the bald lady, I brought, home; she is the one I will be going away with. Somehow, Grandma Lucy; I may be able to return to earth any way. Buy, for now," Peaches says as she will turn to walk away from the grave site now walking home she senses maybe it will be all for the best if *Peach* could depart earth–vacate it all, the prejudice, the police instigation's as well as the entire stench of the city of Baltimore considering, as soon as Peaches returns to the house, she believes of how she may not miss Baltimore–*really, not at all.*

"I have seen the *Milky Way*. My ship passed the beautiful sight, I have ever seen," Lysithea says right now, after eating her pie the alien is somewhat grateful the earth woman had brought along some of Peaches vittles from her world. All the while of Lysithea visit on planet earth especially when, after meeting Peaches next to have a dinner invite from the earth, young lady; Lysithea sense now she is not able to get enough of eating the food of the water globe also the space alien has been feeling little famished.

"How far we have to go?" Peaches ask at the moment, the earth woman is sitting in the chair looking also at all of the many gadgets inside of the spaceship even though Peaches something inside of her wants her to believe as of now; *Peach* is really having a dream. As she listens to Lysithea explains not only the distance but how far she, and Peaches will have to travel all of a sudden, the two women will be interrupted by the sound of the *voice pilot* inside of the spaceship. *WARNING, a sea of giant rocks is moving towards the spaceship, your majesty,* the voice pilot says all of a sudden as the voice pilot warns, Lysithea's spaceship will be almost bombarded by what is known as a meteor shower.

"Who's the majesty?" Peaches ask, right now, both women will cower in a far corner of the spaceship as the flying contraption is reeling to keep control as well as not have Peaches and the alien woman's life in danger. After almost twenty minutes of timing as the meteors of various sizes flies pass the spaceship with several ones bumping into the space craft at once the spaceship will gain the momentum of speed flying pass all of the other planets as well as any other unknown worlds before it will suddenly land directly on the main, wandering star; *Megaclithe.*

"DAMN, you could have killed me," Peaches shouts out at Lysithea as, both women are standing to their feet obviously the danger of the meteor shower is over now.

"I did not," Lysithea's says then now she will ask Peaches to come follow her down the ladder the object is now lowered to Lysithea's domain, her planet.

"We are here already?" Peaches ask not answering the earth woman; Lysithea when, after she has climbed down the ladder; Peaches will hesitate before she decided to step one of her feet on the object when a few minutes of hesitating; Peaches will slowly climb down the ladder right after the extraterrestrial. After climbing down from the spaceship, both women will see a man with three others walking to where Lysithea has landed on the region of *Megaclithe*; as the alien stands there, ready for whatever at the moment, even though Peaches is exhaling and inhaling the freshest air, she has ever breathe more than the atmosphere of Earth when those four men have walked closer; Peaches senses as if she will faint out of sights as the young woman from the earth city of

Baltimore eyes is beholding one of the alien men, who is a good looking, and imposing extraterrestrial.

"Kaysen; I am sorry. I only wanted to make you happy. You have been so sad since the disappearance of mother," Lysithea says as she is now hugging her father Kaysen as Peaches is looking wide-eyed at the group of alien men folks.

"You only did what you wanted to do. We will talk later," the alien by the name of Kaysen says then now he will avert his glance towards *Peaches O' day*, earth woman extraordinary. "The earth woman here?" Kaysen asks.

"Yes. Her name is Peaches, and she has been so kind to me," Lysithea says as she is now still hugging her father. With her legs feeling as if they are made of gelatin, now the monarch of *Megaclithe* will invite Peaches to his palace along with the other aliens men folks as well as Kaysen's daughter Lysithea as the earth woman walks along with her alien hosts; Peaches will avert her glance up towards the starry atmosphere of Megaclithe even now the earth lady from the earth city of Baltimore believes there is a star like constellation in the shape, and form of her now dead, grandmother's face; *Lucille O' day.*

"I must apologize for my daughter; she is, headstrong," the monarch of Megaclithe says to Peaches as the two are now outside of his palace. After almost a week of living on the wandering orb; Peaches has become little accustomed of living on a different world so dissimilar from Peach. At the moment, she smiles as Peaches looks at the man right now she understands as to why she was ushered to Kaysen's world, also Peaches has been invited to the domain of another extraterrestrial, the one name Ninsun the alien, who had almost given up on the return of Lysithea from earth also the Ninsun was little upset because the space being had assumed he would have to suffer the consequences for even allowing Lysithea to board the spaceship and travel to earth all alone.

"Lysithea explained to me why I was chosen. I believe, I may like here on your planet. She also said you as the commander of Megaclithe is able to meet my demands," Peaches says as she will observe in a far distance there are other Megaclithians obviously mingling maybe talking about the earth woman, who has arrived for one obvious reason to marry the commander Kaysen.

"Yes, however only afterwards," Kaysen says as he looks at Peaches, and now he thinks of how well his daughter had chosen seemingly the right like, earth woman to become the commander's bride. "If you are having second assumptions even about me as well as my world–later, I could arrange––," Kaysen says at the moment he will hear of how Peaches, for now will not have any objections.

"I will stay, and wait," Peaches says at the moment she is sensing the warmth, like also a sensuous while talking to the good-looking, alien now walking alongside him as Peaches is again exploring other regions of Megaclithe all the time of her venture on the new world according to the earth woman; Peaches once again will be *warned by the monarch Kaysen to least of all stay away from the restricted area of the planet of where the dead of Megaclithe's souls go there forever.*

"While you were away; I believed your father will have me punished," Ninsun says at the moment as he, and Lysithea are now laying side-by-side on his bed in the house of where Ninsun lives, as well the house the alien hopes he will share with Lysithea one day. Ever since her return to Megaclithe from Earth, the two aliens have sorted of like inseparable even though Lysithea in secret commanded by her father of the time Kaysen wants to occupy with the space woman. Knowingly to Lysithea; she has been pining for the affectionate love from Ninsun all the while the alien was on earth in search for Kaysen a *wife* from the *water globe*. "I could have traveled along with you," Ninsun says at the moment, he will get up slowly out of bed to dress in a silken like robe one of Lysithea's servants had made for the alien.

"No. The mission was for Kaysen. If you had traveled with me; then what?" Lysithea asks as she is sitting up in the bed of Ninsun, her nude body is almost exposed. With no more talk with her alien lover; Lysithea is almost left alone in the house of Ninsun after she dresses, and showers to go as well as met again with the earth woman, and Kaysen; soon as Lysithea is all dressed, and ready to go; Ninsun will apologize for acting little abrupt with the woman he wants to *marry* as well. "I will return with Peaches least for a visit," Lysithea says now she is leaving the house of her alien, love lorn. While she is gone; Ninsun will think of the days, and nights he occupied brooding about Lysithea. Perhaps out of sheer boredom as well she should have traveled along with Ninsun, but early one morning as he was walking outside of his house, Ninsun had decided go out, and

227

walk around Megaclithe all during the time of his wandering, the space being had walked to the area known as the area of the *dead souls' eternity*. All the while of Ninsun standing there at the time, and thinking about Lysithea's tryst on planet Earth all of a sudden, Ninsun had thought he heard the voice of woman in the area crying out his name. Then, thinking of only it is his imagination; Ninsun had turned to go to his house later on a new night as he was trying to go to sleep, it was at the moment Ninsun had heard the shouting of two other aliens. Hurrying outside of his house, Ninsun had looked up towards the atmosphere of Megaclithe to see a bright, illuminating light as the light deemed suddenly Ninsun, and the other extraterrestrials could see Lysithea's approaching, spaceship. Though, he had forgiven Lysithea, perhaps she was little correct. Only deep within him, Ninsun could have found for him a beautiful, earth woman like the one, the monarch of Megaclithe will soon marry; a lady known simply by her home cosmic name; *Peaches*.

"Distance between my world and yours– in time," Lysithea say to Peaches on the evening as the earth woman is preparing for her wedding to Kaysen, the sole monarch of a planet known as Megaclithe. Putting on the various silken like robes, Peaches now understands why the *voice pilot* inside of Lysithea's spaceship at the time the two were traveling throughout space on their way to Lysithea's world, the device made mentioned by saying the word; *majesty.* Meaning then only one, *Peaches O' day* from the greenish, blue globe a terrestrial one almost like Megaclithe.

"Well, your father did promise me; I could go home whenever I so pleases," Peaches says while, now trying on a purple robe like with gold sequins the clothing made by two of the servants of

Lysithea, and Kaysen's household. As Lysithea looks at Peaches getting dressed in her robes of purple and gold sequins, also the alien's eyes are gleaming the shiny, amber shades now Lysithea thinks if only her father had not wanted to marry a woman from earth, the extraterrestrial may have eventually traveled to the water planet for Lysithea's curiosity. "Now, I understand why there were people from my planet, a shade of black like me arrived to Megaclithe all because of the light years ahead. As if you, and the aliens of your world sees way ahead into the future like," Peaches says, even though Lysithea will now sit her legs close together looking at the earth woman within a few hours will become the new mother to the extraterrestrial, even though both women really do not have any qualms regarding to Peaches new out of her world's station in life.

"It is, time," Lysithea says now standing up from the bed inside of the bedroom of the palace of where Peaches has been sleeping since her arrival, before the earth woman and Lysithea go to another area of the palace for the wedding, and feast; Peaches will hug Lysithea. "You are indeed kind," is all the alien says now the two will walk to a room a, much larger one all decorated to the exact there are the attendees the other aliens of Megaclithe. All the time of her smiling, and talking to her new, extraterrestrial kindred, it will be soon time for Peaches and Kaysen to dismiss the guests at their wedding for a night to begin their love even though Peaches will discern little homesickness, however she knows all because of the promise from Kaysen, the new bride and majesty of Megaclithe is able to return home whenever *Peaches O' day* wants to also is prepared.

"This all seems so unreal," Peaches says as she is standing near a window of the wedding chamber, a room especially prepared for the earth woman, and her new groomsmen a alien, who is the commandant of his world; *Megaclithe.*

"It is all real. Your world as well as mine," Kaysen says as he sits on the bed waiting for the moment ever since the earth woman has arrived to his cosmos. As he looks at the loveliness of Peaches even now Kaysen will think of is he is able he could find the many ways he could thank his headstrong daughter, even though Lysithea almost gave him an all, out interstellar shake-up when Kaysen had discovered his daughter had not only built a spaceship, Lysithea had taken all of her initiative travel to earth in search a new bride for her father.

"You love me?" Peaches ask, as she slowly turns away from the window to look at her new husband, a man only Peaches knows if her dear grandma Lucy was still alive and living on Megaclithe, the old, grand matriarch of the O'day family will approve.

"Yes; I do. I loved you when my daughter brought you here. However, there is still the time," now Kaysen has got up from the bridal bed and is now holding Peaches, however with no more words and sensing the urgency to make love even though, while on planet Earth;

Peaches had not had the adventure to choose a man to break opening the *door of felicity* between her now wanting thighs, as she, and Kaysen osculate now Peaches will not wait as she undresses quickly as her new, interstellar husband stands back, and looks at the fine, brown form of his bride from earth. During the sensual moment of she, and Kaysen's rundle between the satin, sheets; after feeling the slight pain of her virginity gone by the way of love from an alien suddenly Peaches will sense the most intimate embrace, as Kaysen with his *moontang*, overblown python moves in, and out of Peaches wet, sticky and wanting *earth like fangita*. Because of her first, loving experience; Peaches O'DAY senses she cannot get enough *la douleur exquise* from her interstellar husband. Now, because of the unrequited love; Peaches will wait for her husband Kaysen when the supernova sets on the plains of Megaclithe, and all during the moments of their heated, *grant salveson* passion between the bed sheets of the married couples bed, the other aliens of Megaclithe seems not to mind whenever the majesty from planet earth will occupy the *desibaba* nights under the stars except those feverish, wild and *throw it in moments* are inside the *Vancouver* bedroom of the palace.

"HELP ME, NINSUN," she scremed on day as she was looking behind a veil like darkness at one her alien kindred, and after screaming again for the space alien name Ninsun; Amenata had given up. She knew after marrying the monarch of Megaclithe not to ever venture not only to close to the forbidden region of the planet of where the dead soul's of an alien goes, and never returns, however Amenata was a little curious really to find out. The time Amenata had walked to the shadowy region of Megaclithe, she had assumed even after walking into the obscure, like

place maybe Kaysen would be forgiving of her. As she walked in slowly, the hazy area had felt cold to Amenata, but she did not really care as she walked as the alien looked only at the eyes of the souls, who are dearly departed; Amenata will sense excitement and sensuous like even though the alien should not concerning the dead of her world.

"I GOT YOU HERE; AT LAST," Amenata had heard a voice like booming in a sense and now looking into the dead like eyes, the at one time majesty of Megaclithe will observe it is her husband's dead nemesis, an alien, who had tried to destroy Kaysen

only to overtake the monarchy of the wandering orb.

"RELEASE ME; I AM THE MAJESTY," Amenata shouts out at the chimera of her husband's nemesis, and as the phantom laughs while seemingly to drag Amenata further, and deeper into the obscure region of the planet now the nemesis has the queen of Megaclithe to the exact of where he wants Amenata. Days after missing from her domain on Megaclithe, the incubus will have his way with the majesty. Dragging Amenata by her slender, like arms to his cavern while there the incubus of the nemesis, who had fought a duel and lost; will have his way *with Amenata's body. Though, his withered and weak hands like pieces of ice, the feel will not deter the specter of the nemesis to make love to Amenata. As his hands move all over her warm body, it is the penetration of his cold, though dead lund boto moving in, and out of Amenata's warm, alien puday as if there is a moment of heated desire between Amenata and the phantom. Every time behind the obscure veil of the forbidden area, the now dead nemesis will have his erotic, moments of the lovemaking with the wife of the alien, who had killed the nemesis. Sometimes, as well as unknowing to her; Amenata will relent to his will even thinking there is some life into the chimera for the reason for his maddening, consensual rape. Then, one day with the incubus nowhere to find her; Amenata had walked to the forbidden opening of the region of the planet only for the dead, and standing there she had seen the alien Ninsun.*

"LEAVE ME BE. ONLY THE LIVING COULD RESCUE ME," Amenata shouts out, however her shouting at the incubus will do her of now account as she again is being dragged back to the cavern of her dead husband's enemy. With the thought to allow the chimera to do his will with her still, living alien body; Amenata will

have a thought to somehow fool the phantom as he is now rubbing his cold, course hands all over her now naked body followed by the incubus again penetrating the alien Amenata making love to her as if the incubus is trying to kill the alien with the act of serraph behind, a murky also forbidden veil of Megaclithe.

A mission for myself, the alien Ninsun thinks when one morning when most of the other extraterrestrials of Megaclithe are asleep possibly because of the celebrations of the monarch Kaysen to the Earth woman known simply as *Peaches;* Ninsun since the arrival of the woman from Earth has been wanting to travel to the globe as of now, as Ninsun is again on his way to an area of where the spaceship he designed as well as built, the alien is more curious to find out more regarding to the water globe right now he looks up at the skies above Megaclithe the planet is already seen and it looks to be closer than previously. *What else is on the world known as Earth? Riches untold?* Ninsun thinks as he keeps walking and no longer looking at the blue, greenish planet glistening like a gem with two shades soon Ninsun will be at the location of where the spaceship is positioned. Now, standing close to the spaceship; Ninsun will say the words for the flying contraption to open, and slowly the door latch opens followed by the lowering of the ladder. The extraterrestrial smiles as he looks at his invention, now climbing up the wooden ladder with the glassy accents, after Ninsun steps inside he will see what looks like possibly bits of food in a far corner of the spaceship. As he looks at the food, Ninsun has a look of disgust across his handsome face because, while sitting down in the chair in front of the mainframe of the spaceship, Ninsun remembers the time Lysithea after her return had told Ninsun all about the different foods then Lysithea had eaten.

With the hopes no other Megaclithians will hear his take off, Ninsun will take, hold of the navigation bar least to stave off the voice pilot since the device inside of the spaceship now only operates the spaceship by the words of the *current* majesty, *Peaches* the woman from planet Earth. Sitting still, all of a sudden the spherical, flying contraption will sputter gently within almost a few minutes of timing, Ninsun will sense the spaceship is starting to gale off into the atmosphere above Megaclithe. All the while of the alien sitting in the chair of the spaceship as the round, object floats gently into orbit before flying full speed; Ninsun is able to hear the shouts, as well as words of the Megaclithians, who has run out of their homes maybe on their way to the area of where the spaceship was positioned, however by the time even the commander of Megaclithe arrives; Ninsun will be on his way traveling through the great beyond on his way to *Earth*.

"NINSUN, WAIT," Lysithea shouts as she is running out of the palace after awakening from the sound of the spaceship as she runs to the area, there is other extraterrestrials trailing in behind the monarch's daughter. By the time Lysithea has arrived to the area, there is only a glimpse of the spaceship as it continues its course all the way into the skies above Megaclithe right now, as the anger is starting to see the inside of Lysithea; she only knows right now Ninsun is inside of the spaceship possibly on his way to Earth. While standing there looking up until the flying ship is no longer seen now Kaysen has arrived with his new espouse, Peaches.

"What is happening?" Peaches ask as she is looking at her husband Kaysen and the man appears not to be well pleased perhaps of what has happened. As she, and Kaysen listens to Lysithea explains Ninsun has taken off in the spaceship right now it will be the wife of the new monarch, who will become a little upset. Although Peaches is placed as like the new queen to Kaysen; she has been discerning the alien by the name of Ninsun would probably pull such an act because at the time of her wedding to Kaysen, the certain alien all the while was questioning Peaches about Earth.

"Your world seems fascinating," Ninsun had said during the ceremony while sitting next to Peaches, and Kaysen.

"Full of troubles, and turmoil's when I left. Until I came here, and found out your world now mine; is many light years away," Peaches told Ninsun, as she is looking up at the sky even though the spaceship cannot be seen any longer, the earth woman is starting to sense the shivers on the mere thought of how Ninsun is now on his way to Earth without any notion of the dangers he could possibly confront.

"The ship belongs only to me. It is to be used only for my return to Earth-someday," Peaches says right now she will observe during the upsetting moment, her alien lover, and husband and now friend is becoming more disquieted.

"He could crash. There is a device only hears by our new queen," Lysithea says right now she will explain to her father Kaysen when all the time Lysithea was traveling in outer space on her way to Earth; there inside of the flying ship was a mechanisms will hear every word Lysithea will say literally to guide her to the water globe.

"I hate to say these words; if Ninsun do not arrives to Earth safely; he got what he deserved by not obeying my queen," Kaysen says then now he will ask his daughter Lysithea if she knows of any other way to rebuild a new spaceship since it had been his only child's idea. As she moves her head to show Lysithea do not have no notion whatsoever, suddenly in the midst of the first family of Megaclithe another alien will say of how she do know regarding to the building of the spaceship.

"I do know, Kaysen. I worked with Ninsun with the design as well as what materials to use," the alien by the name of Jasmine says right now Peaches while standing there will observe of how lovely the extraterrestrial by the name jasmine is; tall, deep mahogany shade and although her head as neatly shaven as the other females of Megaclithe, it is the shape of Jasmine's eyes enchantingly, almond shaped and her mouth is curved, and full having the alien Jasmine to be even more *alluring*.

"Then later, on the command of my queen; you will be ready to design a new ship and I will have as many workers as you will need," is all Kaysen says right now he and his *fresh* queen Peaches are leaving the area of where the last, new spaceship was located. Now, Jasmine and Lysithea will talk about the monarch's new wife, one of whom Jasmine hopes will be appreciative of the alien when the times arrives for the new queen making ready to return to Earth.

"When the moment comes; I aim to please our new queen," Jasmine says as she is looking at the new queen walking alongside her husband, the commander of Megaclithe; Kaysen. "I truly understand why Ninsun decided to take off to visit the queen's planet."

"Ninsun has no idea of how dangerous earth is now. Our world is so many light years ahead of Earth," Lysithea says now Jasmine will talk more with Lysithea mainly about the extraterrestrial's mother, who had disappeared behind a shadowy, veil of where only the deceased of Megaclithe are sent.

"Your mother and I was good friend. She protected me after my parents had gone to the forbidden area of Megaclithe,"

Jasmine says leaving Lysithea a little clueless because of all the years Amenata was around before her sudden disappearance, the at one time wife of Kaysen never did mention of another alien by the name of Jasmine, who Amenata had befriended. With no more words spoken between Lysithea as well as Jasmine, the two extraterrestrials will go to their individual home sadly for the remainder of the day almost until Ninsun returns, Lysithea will stay almost brooding because of Ninsun's absence-least until one day, Lysithea will have the alien Jasmine to come to her home out of a goodwill like reason.

My opportunity, the alien Jasmine thinks while she is in her home, now all alone when, after living there with her parents, who had died and their souls are everlasting behind a veil on Megaclithe. As she is sitting in one of the rooms of her house all of a sudden a flood of memories will enter the extraterrestrial's head of the time Jasmine had recalled when Kaysen's last queen; Amenata had gone missing only possibly to assume Amenata could have gone right to the forbidden zone of the planet. "I am sorry," Jasmine had said to Kaysen when one afternoon, the alien had walked to the palace to observe Kaysen was indeed sorrowful. "May I help you with what you need?" She has asked, at the moment Kaysen had stood up to tell Jasmine perhaps another time all because the monarch needed even at the time to be alone; as well as think. After what will turn into like days on end, one warm night on Megaclithe; Jasmine will have a visitor. When she opened the door to her house there standing the commander of Megaclithe; Kaysen. She was almost speechless when she had seen him standing there next ushering Kaysen into the home where the two space inhabitants talked for hours at the moment, Jasmine had assumed she would become the next in line to become the espouse of Kaysen.

"Is it not good, for our *master* to be so alone?" Jasmine asked during the certain moment, also at the time she was standing behind the monarch as Kaysen was sitting in one her chairs also Jasmine was caressing, Kaysen's full, mane like ponytail.

"There is a way to see to my loneliness. The visitors here from a world known as Earth have given me and consideration," Kaysen said then Jasmine had stopped suddenly her caressing of the monarch's full, ponytail. With no more words said afterwards, Jasmine had found her to be almost jilted or maybe she had not been too truthful regarding to her love for her commander of Megaclithe. Now, the like opportunity has arrived perhaps by the coincidence another alien of the planet has gone off to Earth in the new queen's spaceship thereby having Jasmine a new time to rebuild for the new majesty, an Earth woman by the name of *Peaches*. Suddenly, knock on Jasmine's front door of her house will jolt the alien out of her dreams of what ifs. Walking to the door and opening it slowly standing on the other side of it is one of the main workers, who helped Jasmine and Ninsun with the construction of the now departed also gone away spaceship, the space *inhabitant* name Moswen.

"You sent for me?" He asks his hair tied in the same way as most of the men of Megaclithe also Moswen is as tall likewise he has broad shoulders befitting of like a builder on the plenum.

"We have work to do soon; Moswen," Jasmine says as she will usher the alien inside of her home right now, Jasmine is feeling some thermal, sensual feelings for Moswen most of all be came to Jasmine's brooding when the monarch of the cosmos Megaclithe had pushed away Jasmine's advances. Now, as she and Moswen are sitting inside of her house;

Jasmine will explain in detail of what could be anew project is; make ready to build a new spaceship for the new Earth queen by the name of Peaches. As she looks into the eyes of Moswen, right now Jasmine will recall when the first time, she had met Moswen. Not only the builder of the cosmos proven to be like a stand in lover for Jasmine, however it was what Moswen had told Jasmine one night when the two were exhausted from a new night of the sexual, heat of blue shifting between the sheets of Jasmine's bed. Caressing her *pudenda* as he talked; Moswen talked of the time he had walked through the shadowy, veil of the forbidden zone only to be encountered by the force, that keeps the souls of the dead inside of the barred area.

"Its' called the *goliwok*. Though I was not dead at the time; I made a bargain with the *goliwok*. If it would set me free; I will bring to the *goliwok* anyone living alien for his desire," Moswen said with a malicious like grin across his deep, brown though handsome face.

"You did not do of what I'm thinking?" Jasmine asked with her full, yet satisfied body exposed to the one alien, she believes she may occupy her lonely nights on Megaclithe–least until at the moment. As she listens in like a horror despite the fact she has now enjoyed a night of the *jany* acts with Moswen; Jasmine had learned of how Moswen had lured Amenata somewhat to the forbidden zone. At the torment, with the traitor of sorts in her house, Jasmine will tell Moswen there will be other plans regarding to the building of the new spaceship for queen *Peaches*.

"Is there more?" Moswen asks his masculine, galactic is becoming more alluring to Jasmine.

"I will send for you later," Jasmine says right now she is standing to show to the alien; otherwise.

"How about a serving of that space tea?" Moswen says right now he has walked over to where a bar like, set of furniture inside the house of Jasmine at the moment reaching for the jug of what is known as the planets' most intoxicating liquor, the extraterrestrial with the broad like shoulders will pour for him a glassy, like goblet of the space tea–the drink, cold tasty and sweet so delicious, the new queen has ordered more jugs of the drink in her palace for the time when *Peaches*, and Kaysen entertains guests to the place. At the moment, the more Moswen drinks of the elixir, the more Jasmine will see of how the builder is becoming intoxicated. It will not be for too long, Jasmine with her slim, tall legs high in the air as she is laying underneath Moswen is feeling his overblown, throbbing *manhood* banging all inside of Jasmine's vulva, *peachy* colored now saturating with juices of lovemaking and when their moment is over, after Moswen departs her house; Jasmine realizes at times she must relent to the *rompish* advances of the main builders of Megaclithe, for after all of what he knows concerning the disappearance of the last *ruler* of Megaclithe; *Amenata*, it could be the death of both Jasmine also Moswen.

Days after Ninsun's escape it looks from Megaclithe in a spaceship, Ninsun had built for Lysithea though she is grateful her father Kaysen has married a woman from planet Earth; if only Ninsun had waited maybe Lysithea could have traveled along with her lovelorn. While in her bedroom, Lysithea thinks of what terrible fate Ninsun could confront all the time he is on Earth, such as if Ninsun had landed on the identical area of where Lysithea had landed when she visited Earth. With no more thoughts if Ninsun will be safe all of a sudden, Lysithea will hear her queen now stepmother Peaches call out for the extraterrestrial. Now, walking to the dining hall of where her father Kaysen is waiting, Lysithea will observe of how beautifully decorated her stepmother has redesigned the room in the palace.

"Jasmine came by to visit. Your stepmother did not want to awake you," Kaysen says appearing like years younger since the marriage to the earth woman, Peaches. Regarding to the jargon to identify when a woman marries a man be he an alien or, otherwise, also the man have children; stepmother, both the monarch of Megaclithe also his daughter had learned the earth vocabulary from Peaches; respectfully.

"I will go to her house. She wants to talk about building another spaceship for our new queen," Lysithea says even though she is sensing maybe Kaysen thinks his daughter may want the new flying ship for her use to go after Ninsun since the alien has been away. "Do not worry," Lysithea says as he looks at Kaysen when, after eating her morning meal; Lysithea will go to visit Jasmine also promising her new, stepmother and the now new queen of Megaclithe of when Lysithea will be returning home because Peaches wants to explore more of her new plenum.

This has to work, jasmine thinks as she is looking out of the window of her house to see the monarch and new queen's daughter is walking to Jasmine's humbled, galactic dwelling. The reason Jasmine thinks of what may work is all because Jasmine has been knowing of how the pass queen Amenata had ended behind the shadowy veil on the other area of the cosmos of where the dead of Megaclithe to go until all eternity. A concept Jasmine is now aware of is what the alien had found out from her lover Moswen, an incubus like creature on the planet of Megaclithe known as a *goliwok*. To now, think of the creature, living in the restricted zone for its evil like purpose is having the extraterrestrial skin of Jasmine to crawl with a cold like sensation. As soon as Lysithea is close enough to Jasmine's house, the designer of the last spaceship will go out and meet the monarch's daughter.

"Your new mother told me; you were asleep when I came over," Jasmine says as she looks at Lysithea right now Jasmine only imagines of how good it is for the monarch's daughter. Mainly because Jasmine in lieu of the fact her dear parents are now gone to their souls wandering behind the gloomy, like veil on Megaclithe, however Jasmine senses she must tell Lysithea of possibly of what might have happened to Lysithea's mother; Amenata.

"And, I want to know the reason," Lysithea says then now Jasmine will have Lysithea to come along with her so the two will walk to the forbidden area of Megaclithe. After arriving, Lysithea will look at Jasmine suspiciously like all because of the law Kaysen has placed out literally regarding to the gloomy region of Megaclithe. "Why are we here?" Lysithea asks now she is showing a fiery like glint in her beautiful, amber shade of eyes the feature Lysithea is known to exhibit most of all when the extraterrestrial is *incensed*.

"I am here to confess," Jasmine says, now the alien will talk and tell Lysithea of what Jasmine had learned if by chance the monarch's daughter mother could be held captive behind the shadowy veil. "My dear Moswen; I do not believe he wanted to harm your mother," Jasmine lastly say.

"YOU TWO WILL BE HELD AS TRAITORS," Lysithea screams at Jasmine almost frightening her however, the two are so close to what looks to be the opening of the gloomy, like veil of the region of Megaclithe the shout will startle something behind the obscure, like veil at the moment both aliens will see a long, stringy gray hand reach out and the aim of the hand will grab one of Jasmine's slender, like arms having Jasmine to now scream out for help. "Hang onto me; now," Lysithea says to instruct Jasmine to grab a hold of one of Lysithea's hand to stop whatever is trying to grab a hold of Jasmine to drag the alien into the gloomy, like region of Megaclithe.

"I CANNOT BREATHE," Jasmine is now shouting out as she tries to take a hold of one of Lysithea's hands to stop whatever is trying to kidnapped Jasmine into the forbidden zone. As the two aliens will struggle, and pull it seems as if the hidden, strong like force has more strength than the two extraterrestrials. As the two are fighting and struggling all of a sudden also slowly Jasmine's body will be sucked into the gloomy region at the moment as Lysithea is sensing fear; she will hear the screams and shouts of Jasmine slowly fading as the alien is trapped behind the shadowy veil. Standing stills now, Lysithea will sense if she do not return to the area of where the other *Megaclithians* are living as well as to her father, and Lysithea's Earth mother Peaches to warn everyone of what has happened, then of whatever is inside of the gloomy, shadow may reach out to snatch Lysithea. Before she turns and runs to the area of where the other aliens are; Lysithea will hear a soft, sound the voice like of her mother Amenata when she would call out Lysithea was even a smaller alien.

"Lysithea, Lysithea," the voice whispers however, because of the fear as well as agitation Lysithea is sensing after losing the one alien kindred behind of what is the danger zone of Megaclithe as soon as Lysithea arrives to her home, she will take, note Kaysen and Peaches the earth mother is standing outside with four

other aliens, one of whom Lysithea will learn is the one known as Moswen, the extraterrestrial, who may be responsible of what has happened to Lysithea's mother Amenata.

"What is wrong my child?" Kaysen asks Lysithea at the moment the alien daughter is hugging her father, and Lysithea's body is shaking as she is sobbing out of controllably.

"Kaysen; she is hysterical," Peaches says as she is looking at her stepdaughter, and although the Earth woman agreed to return to Megaclithe with Lysithea to become a bride to the extraterrestrial's father; as of now Peaches thinks as she looks at Lysithea shaking as she is crying what if something more menacing is transforming on Megaclithe, also if the earth woman Peaches will be able to withstand? Now, pulling away from her father to talk; Lysithea will tell the horrifying story of what has happened to Jasmine as well as, who is the culprit in behind Amenata disappearance behind a shadowy, forbidden like area of Megaclithe. While listing to his daughter Lysithea unknowingly to the other aliens including the monarch of the planet as well as Lysithea, the space inhabitant by the name of Moswen will take off with a sprint to the prohibited zone.

"Moswen is the alien responsible for it all?" Peaches ask as she is looking at the alien Moswen running with all of his speed as he is on his way to the certain region.

"Lysithea; stay here with Peaches. I am coming after the traitor," Kaysen says right now there will be least ten other alien men folks, who have gathered around because of the commotion also those ten are following the monarch of Megaclithe to the restricted range.

"Be care. There is a creature behind the veil, the *goliwok*," Lysithea says as Peaches looks at her alien, stepdaughter, however, before the sun sets on

Megaclithe even though the monarch Kaysen along with ten other alien, men folks have not returned; Peaches as she is sitting outside of the palace with her stepdaughter Lysithea will learn of what a *goliwok* is; a creature likes, who lives behind the shadowy veil of where the forbidden region of Megaclithe.